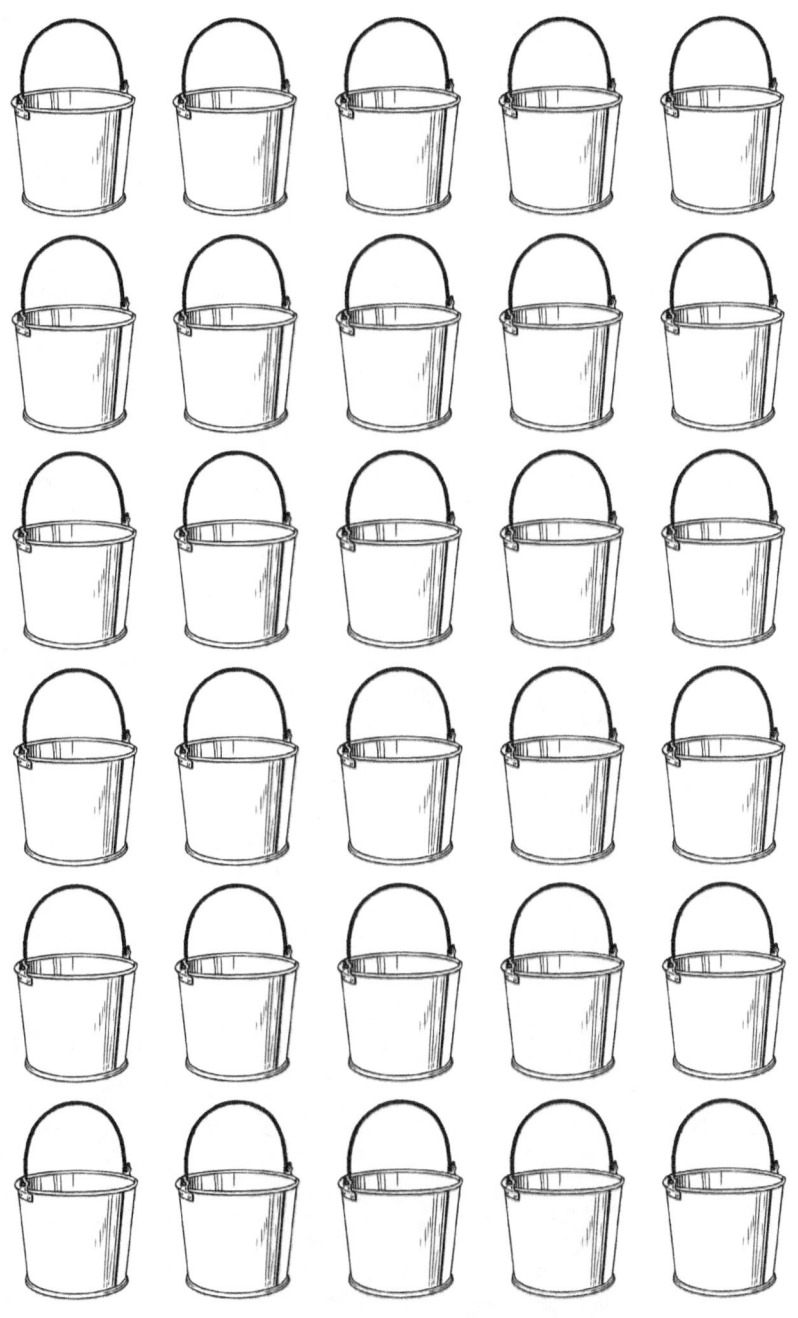

Pure Slush Books

2014

April

Vol. 4

a Pure Slush book

Pure
Slush

April 2014 Vol. 4 is edited by Matt Potter and
published by Pure Slush, January 2014.

All stories are copyright © of the individual authors

Cover photograph copyright © of Florin Garoi
http://500px.com/floringaroi

ISBN: 978-1-925101-27-0

You can find *Pure Slush* at http://pureslush.webs.com

Copies of all *Pure Slush* publications can be bought
at http://pureslush.webs.com/store.htm

All queries re *Pure Slush* can be made
via email to edpureslush@live.com.au

A note on differences in punctuation and spelling

Pure Slush proudly features (both online and in print) writers from all over the English-speaking world. Some speak and write English as their first language, while for others, it's their second or third or even fourth language. Naturally, across all versions of English, there are differences in punctuation and spelling, and even in meaning. These differences are reflected in the stories *Pure Slush* publishes, and it accounts for any differences in punctuation, spelling and meaning found within these pages.

stories by

Guilie Castillo-Oriard

James Claffey

Townsend Walker

Gwendolyn Joyce Mintz

Derek Osborne

Stephen V. Ramey

Gloria Garfunkel

Gay Degani

John Wentworth Chapin

Sally-Anne Macomber

Lynn Beighley

Mandy Nicol

Andrew Stancek

Margaret Bingel

Rachel Ambrose

Darryl Price

Gill Hoffs

Teresa Burns Gunther

Susan Tepper

Matt Potter

Jessica McHugh

Gary Percesepe

Shane Simmons

Nathaniel Tower

Michelle Elvy

Kimberlee Smith

Len Kuntz

Vanessa Weibler Paris

Michael Webb

Joanne Jagoda

for

Sally-Anne

… thanks for the rescue

M.P.

The Hunt for Pélagie Solak

by Guilie Castillo-Oriard

The inside of Luis Villalobos's Rubicon Jeep feels like an oven preheated for the Christmas turkey, even with the air conditioning at full blast. "Ultra powerful compressor," the salesman said back in December. "Special for Curaçao." Four months later, barely spring, and the island heat has already defeated it.

And Milena – his boss, his lover – has defeated Luis.

As he parks outside the ironwork gate of #74 Jan Sofat, his phone buzzes in one of the central console's cubbyholes. Milena. He's tempted to lower the window and throw the damn thing into the mangroves.

How *could* she?

And how could *he* have been so trusting? Like a fool – so apropos today – he'd been celebrating. A year's worth of compliance work achieved in two months, just in time to meet the FATCA deadline next week. Failure would cost Ehrlich Fiduciary its license. And Luis his righteousness, after all the confrontations with Milena.

But he never expected her to pull rank, go behind his back. Or Wendolyn to fall in with it.

Wendolyn looking at Julissa, her assistant. Julissa looking at the floor. Comprehension beginning to crack wide open. Discovering Wendolyn's loyalties hurt, but what really rankled was her justification – a shabby *It's just six*

15

entities, Luis. Only one is domiciled in Curaçao. She sounded just like Milena.

He locates a bell next to the gate, rings it twice. Six days to fix this. He'll do it himself. No one else can be trusted.

A huge uniformed maid surrounded by a dozen dogs is shouting to make herself heard over the barking. "I already said, sir. Ms. Solak not home."

"When will she be back?"

The dogs push bared teeth through the suddenly-flimsy-looking iron bars. The maid – Jamaican, judging by how her vowels stretch like putty – shrugs. "She have no schedule when she out with the dogs."

Luis eyes the canine Dawn of the Dead swarming the gate. "*More* dogs?"

The maid narrows her eyes. "You not know Ms. Solak well, do you, sir? What business you have to see her about so urgently? You selling something?"

"No, I'm not selling anything. It's – confidential." But he knows he won't make a dent on this Amazon. Besides, he's got a hunch. "Please ask her to call me."

His business card disappears into the folds of the Jamaican's apron. Back inside the sweltering Jeep, Luis makes a note to request heavier paper for his business cards. Something that might provide a full minute of chewing pleasure for a dog.

Weekday car rides mean only one thing for Al. Luis catches him throwing suspicious glances his way from the back seat. "No, bud, no vet. A little work for me first, and I'm hoping you'll help me with that. Then straight-up fun. Sound good?"

Luis heard of this dog beach last month, has been meaning to bring Al. If there's any cosmic justice, he'll find the elusive Ms. Solak here, no gatekeepers except her dogs. Surely she won't sic them on a fellow pet owner? Without the suit and tie, she won't suspect who he is until it's too late. He has the affidavit in the glove compartment.

One signature is all he needs.

A dirt road ends at an inlet cradled between the hillocks of the St. Joris valley. A Ford Explorer, red under the mud spatters, is parked next to a burst of mangroves. That's the only sign of human presence – Ms. Solak's, Luis hopes. Everything else is red dust and brambly vegetation. The surf laps at gritty shores with lake-like softness, hardly audible above the bluster of wind that slams the Jeep's door back on Luis's shin.

"Carajo!" He smothers the more violent curses, limps out and opens the back, hooks the leash to Al's collar. "Come on, bud."

Al's front legs are splayed, head hanging low, ears flat. His haunches are quivering. A lamb next in line for slaughter couldn't look more pitiful.

"Nothing to be scared of, man. It's the beach! Lots of room to run. You *like* running. And the water – nice, cool water – Aw, come on, Al."

Luis tugs on the leash, but Al wiggles back farther and farther until he's pressed against the passenger-side door. When Luis switches to that side, Al backs away to the driver's side. Finally Luis climbs in, intending to bodily force Al's fifty pounds out of the car.

But the dog's whole body is quaking like the worst case of Parkinson's.

"Hey, buddy. Hey. What's wrong?"

Al whines.

Luis holds Al's massive, shaking body against his chest until the quaking comes only in bursts. Then he reaches for his cigarettes. "Bad idea, huh?"

Another whine.

He lowers all the windows, opens the doors on the downwind side in the unlikely case Al decides the world isn't as scary as it seems. He lights up in the shelter of the car and steps out.

Al's whine is pure anxiety now.

"I'm right here. Just stretching my legs. I'd never leave you – Oh."

The dog is peering out of the car at him, head so far down his nose brushes the seat upholstery.

"Is that it? Someone abandoned you?"

Al's ear twitches.

"That's how you ended up a stray, bud?"

But Al isn't listening. Not to him, anyway. Something out by the bay has caught his attention. Then Luis hears it too. Dogs barking. A whistle. He follows Al's gaze and sees six, maybe seven dogs splashing along the shore three hundred meters away. Behind them walks a figure so slight it might be a child. "That can't be Pélagie Solak. I'm sorry, Al. I put you through all this for nothing."

A barking pack won't help Al's anxiety attack. They better leave before the Ford's owner gets back. He closes the doors, turns the ignition, buckles his seatbelt. "We'll try again tomorrow, okay? Maybe we'll have better luck –"

A scrabble of nails on upholstery, a shift in the Jeep's suspension, a flash of black streaking toward the bay.

"Al! No!"

He forgot about the windows.

The dog is racing for the pack, leash streaming out behind him. Low growling carries back to Luis on the wind. They'll tear him to pieces.

"Al! Get back here!"

Damn suicidal dog. He turns the ignition off, lunges out – shit, the seatbelt. Buckle seems stuck, the band of nylon weave tangles in his arms. Then he's out, tripping over his feet, wishing he could fly. "Al!"

He's not going to reach him in time. Luis watches in horror, legs pumping as if of their own volition, as the pack engulfs Al with a roar.

A whistle, then a single booming HEY!

Luis and the pack – even Al – freeze. The girl – Luis makes out the hint of breasts in the dog owner's tank top – holds up a hand. Like the miracle of bread loaves, her seven beasts, now tame, back off. She approaches Al. The tip of his tail wags. She scratches his chest, takes his leash.

She's small, wiry, no curves worth mentioning. Her face isn't beautiful, not like Milena's or Wendolyn's – no trace of even the memory of make-up, no sexy lips, no come-hither eyes. The skin is freckled, but the bone structure underneath has aristocratic haughtiness. With a shock, Luis realizes this 'girl' is older than him.

The dogs reach him first. He steels himself, but they barely sniff at his feet before moving on. The woman watches him, waits until she's within arm's length before speaking. "Your dog?"

"Yes." Luis tastes tears in his throat, wants to kick his wimpy self. "Thank you. And – I'm sorry. I didn't – he was terrified, didn't want to get out of the car, and then he suddenly –"

She rubs Al behind the ears before handing over the end of his leash. "He was trying to protect you."

Al licks his hand, looks contrite. Later there'll be teary hugs, but right now Luis's macho pride pushes for sassy nonchalance. "Thanks, bud, but I can take care of myself."

The woman doesn't even smile.

Luis wipes the stupid grin off his face, offers a chastised hand. "I'm, uh, Luis."

She looks at it the way one looks at a plate of cookies after two servings of carrot cake. Luis gets the feeling she has no qualms of politeness; he won't be the first, or the last, to be so slighted. When she does give her tiny –

surprisingly strong – grip, he feels the elation of having been found worthy.

"You risked your dog's life to find me, Mr. Villalobos?"

"How do you know my –"

"Francelle called."

"Who's Francelle?"

The woman smiles for the first time. "You met her at my house."

The ground is cracking under his feet. *"You're –"*

"Pélagie Solak, yes. I'll do you the courtesy – no, I'll do your dog the courtesy of listening to whatever you have to say. And then you will leave. Me. Alone."

La Ronde / Annie and Myron

by Townsend Walker

It's three o'clock. Annie sweeps through her office door at PricewaterhouseCoopers, raincoat trailing on the floor. Lunch with Joey ran over. Not lunch as much as finding ways to appropriately thank him for the diamond and emerald bracelet. They both limped out of Room 634 at the Hilton, tired out after three hours lying down.

She pulls out her compact, checks her hair, smooths down her skirt, props up the collar of her blouse. Message light is dancing disjointedly, her assistant pops around the corner, primly announces, "Your client has been waiting," the phone rings.

"Sweetheart baby," the receiver booms.

It's Myron, *Sweetheart baby* is his tag for everyone.

"Where've you been Cuddles? Tenth time I've called."

Annie thinks he only uses "Cuddles" with her, but with Myron, who knows?

"Just got into town, you free tonight?"

Shit. Of all nights, she was planning a long bath looking at her Cartier Panthere through the bubbles.

"Sure, sure, jammed right now. Call you back."

Annie's client, an undersized guy compensating with obvious platform shoes, stumbles through the door carrying two boxes, paper falling out in a trail behind him.

"You said you needed everything, here it is."

"Mr. Johnson, I said I need everything from 2013, not since the company started."

He shrugs – weighed down by boxes, and from his expression, a heavy ennui.

"Just give them to me, I'll have someone sort through it."

Annie resented the partners in Newark foisting this local chain, *Dynamic Mechanics*, on her when she arrived from Los Angeles last year. 2014 would be the first and last year for this account. Not that Joey's moving company is much larger, but Joey has contacts and that ineffable something else (she just spent three hours with).

She calls her assistant in, dumps the boxes on him, then calls Myron.

"Great hearing, Myron. You couldn't tell me you were coming?"

"Wanted to surprise you, baby. Here for a month. Finalizing script, checking out locations, getting a feel for Jersey. We're going to see a lot of one another, if you know what I mean," followed by a chuckle.

Myron is a film producer – a cut above B, but not far. PwC is his studio's accountant, as a favor to the Weinsteins. Myron started out with Bob and Harvey; some people soar, others jog. But Myron knows people; they like him, feel unthreatened by his infrequent successes. He introduced Annie around and helped her firm build up a good clientele in the industry. She came to Newark because there was a partner slot open a year down the road; there wasn't in LA.

§

Annie goes home, power naps, showers, dresses (small, black, not too provocative, as if Myron needs help, or she, around him).

Myron's got this tip from a friend for the Adega Grill. Friend of a friend knows the owner, Carlos Lopes. A corner table, low lights, soft yellow walls, Mediterranean feel. *Quiet, so you can talk.*

"It's been a while, Cuddles. Did you miss me?"

He puts his arm around her. He's the stocky sort, put together out of sausages; all curves no angles and his arm more lies on her shoulder than holds it. Surprisingly agile though, Annie's always thought.

"Of course I did, you big lunk."

Myron has a pretty face for a guy, smooth pink skin, twinkly blue eyes shining on her. "So tell me what's up, not the business, talk to me about you, how's my little Annie liking it out here?"

"There's this deal I can use your help with." She moves in closer to him and drops her voice.

"Say the word."

"Client / friend-getting-to-be: his sister is tight with a woman she went to high school, college, worked with, you know like they've been together forever."

"Yeah, yeah." He moves closer to her too, but for other reasons.

"Her husband beats the crap out of her regularly and she wants to get him offed."

"Offed?" Myron shrugs and squinches up his face.

"Offed." Annie is fairly matter-of-fact about arranging a hit job. She's not sure why.

"Where do I come in?"

"You're a friend of Max, who, I've been told, knows people who know people who might be of service to this lady."

The waiter brings a bottle of Dom Perignon. "From Senhor Lopes. He can't be here tonight, but he's told us to take good care of you."

"Didn't I tell you I had an in?"

"So, you see Max lately?"

"Here's the word on Max." Now Myron is whispering. "Got this from an acquaintance in Tijuana. Max is not a person anyone wants to talk about, and me, I don't know a thing. Last deal did not go down well, some Colombians became very upset with our Max, who as you remember also had some Asian connections and may now be either in the jungles of Burma, or if he didn't get that far, is under 60 feet of water off Catalina."

"Good champagne, let's drink to Max."

Conversation stops as the waiter approaches with a plate of calamari. "The first item on the Chef's tasting menu, Lulas a Romana. Bom apetite!"

"So this client you're getting to be friends with: what's his name?"

Annie is hoping Max doesn't get too inquisitive about Joey. Thoughts of the afternoon, feel of Joey's hands, weight of the bracelet. She's not sure she can pull off blasé at the moment. "Joe Leone. Owns a big moving business. Grew up in the area, contacts everywhere." *Maybe that'll justify Joey for Myron.*

"Leone, Leone. Where'd I hear that name before?"

"So you know someone can help this lady?

Two waiters arrive with the fish course, Bacalhau à Adega Grill, fried salt cod with fresh tomato sauce, sautéed onions, shrimp, Spanish sausage, green peppers and bacon. Max sticks his nose in the platter. "Jezzus, is there anything not in this dish?"

"I can't believe someone here in Jersey can't do the job." He waves a fork full of sausage in the air. "You need to go to the Coast for this."

"Might be better though it's not someone local, hides the trail."

"Well, just so happens ..." Myron takes the pregnant pause and fills his mouth with cod.

"That's fantastic! Joey will be so happy." Annie bounces up and down on the banquette.

"Joey?" Myron sputters, cod sticking to his chin. "It sounds like more than getting-to-be-friends."

"Don't get me wrong, you big bear. Joe, Joey, what's it matter? Don't worry."

Myron sits up, takes Annie's hand, squeezes it (harder than affection would call for), glares at her. "I'm not gonna worry, for the next month anyway, then I'll get you moved back to the Coast. That crowd you work for owe me."

Annie's thinking: just when she and Joey are getting close and even making some wispy plans; he's talked about leaving his wife; the bracelet was not cheap, like 50K at least. Not the sort of thing you give to someone you don't plan to spend some time with anyway. Plus, she figures he's into something that's not in the accounts she's seeing. Searching for a stall or at least time away from Myron: "You know it's tax season and I'm working nights and weekends most of the month."

"We'll find time, Cuddles, we'll find time. Leave it to me."

"Can we get back to the hit man this poor beaten up lady in New York needs? Well, actually she's not too poor, offering fifty for the job."

Annie digs in her purse and pulls out a wadded-up slip of paper (*can't be too careful*); recites in a low monotone: "Guy's name is Franklin Lancaster Cabot III; goes by Frank. Works at Goldman Sachs on West Street, downtown Manhattan. Six foot three, 200 pounds, pasty complexion, curly black hair going gray, beak for a nose, Brooks Brothers dresser, loafers with tassels. And Hermes ties, the silly patterned ones. Outside, Prada Aviators, high-end sunglasses, blue tint even in the rain."

"Okay, I got that. But I don't want to hear about this moving guy any more. Seems too small a fish for you, anyway."

"Sure Myron, sure, count on it."

"That's my Cuddles."

Back in her apartment, and alone, Annie texts Joey: "Max in Burma. Found another lead. Gave him a full description (pasty faced, Brooks, shades, etc)."

Joey picks up as the phone vibrates. *Hell,* he thinks, as he reads her message. *Never did tell her the guy is a tanning bed freak.*

Skullduggery

by Derek Osborne

Max didn't tell her about the cancer that night down in Annapolis. He didn't get back to the boat until well after 2AM. The drive from Manhattan took hours. When he came aboard, all the lights were off except for the navigation lamps. Eddie must have turned them on. Rebecca wasn't curled up on the sofa in the salon as he'd imagined, she was in his cabin, sleeping under the patch-work quilt his kids had made for their mother, her dark hair a jumble over the pillows. She stirred when he bent to kiss her and then she kissed him and then it seemed they were there at the airport, two days later, saying goodbye in the car.

There just wasn't time.

As Rebecca promised, *Miami Blue* is taking another break. She's flown out again, this time commercial, they chartered a chopper from Logan Airport and it's well past midnight. She and Anja are having fun getting smuggled onto the island, the airstrip deserted, only the soft glow of the moon casting shadows down Orange Street, the line of little white shops silent as the jeep's tires rattle over the cobblestone. *Gadabout's* tender waits at the foot of the ramp.

"Skullduggery," Rebecca says as Max quietly rows out to the boat. He's bundled them up in sets of red foul weather gear, only their eyes peeking out.

"We're doing skullduggery."

There's something about climbing onto the big wooden boat in the dead of night. Eddie is there at the rail, helping them with the ladder. With his dreadlocks and deep dark skin, a gold ring in one ear, he looks like a pirate. Max and Rebecca practically run to the cabin.

It's late in the day now and they have barely seen the sun. They've come out of the cabin once for lunch and once for tea. Anja and Eddie are playing cook and concierge; they've come back with groceries and souvenirs and now they've gone out again. The salon mantle is covered with tiny lighthouses and hand-painted birds, hats and tee-shirts strewn on the sofa. There's still an issue with the film company that chartered the boat, their shooting schedule delayed again. Part of why they're out of bed is so Max can find the agreement. Rebecca is modeling some of the tees; she's hard to ignore. Max is on the phone reminding the studio they have to pay for the layover. He goes forward and holds the SAT phone down near the anchor winch, pressing a big black button.

"Hear that, Murray? That's the sound of my anchor coming on board." Rebecca has followed him into the locker, a room full of lines and chain. It's one place they still haven't christened. Murray, the studio's guy, agrees to wire the money that day.

Max is feeling okay. Between the Red Bull, Viagra and pain pills his symptoms have disappeared. He's waiting to start the next round of meds once Rebecca goes back to LA. This time they'll be apart almost two months. The doctors warned him not to abuse the regimen during these rallies but he can't help it, he's one of those guys who are naturally fit, born with pecs and a six-pack, a full head of hair (so far, so good), he doesn't look fifty-six. Eddie calls him 'The Marlboro Man'. Last time Max met with his care team they warned him again. He wanted to ask, "What would you do with Rebecca Vasquez standing naked in front of your bed?"

She's standing there now, just across the cabin, light from the one oil lamp casting its shadows, the curves and lines of her body soaking into the dark wood trims. And yes, she's naked. She hasn't brushed her hair and she doesn't have any tan-lines. He loves the two dimples just above her hips, loves kissing them, loves moving down and hearing her sigh. She comes from a place so deep at times he swears it's another dimension.

"What are these?" she says, opening one of the little drawers over the desk. There's a line of seven stretching across like you'd find in an antique roll-top. Each time they make love she gets up soon after and starts to explore. It's why they've had sex in almost every part of the boat.

And it's quiet now out in the harbor. The Newport crowd has gone home. If it had been full season the four of them might have risked having dinner in town, but things are still a bit thin, none of the restaurant lines you'd find in summer. An odd dynamic, safety in numbers, celebrity sightings expected there on Nantucket. "Too much exposure," Anja decided. Seeing her boss disappointed she added, "We'll do takeout." The reason she and Eddie went back ashore.

Rebecca wanted skullduggery.

"The drawers are part of the legend," Max says.

She's holding one of them up to the lamp, exposing the curve of her breast. The drawer is small, the width of a wallet and not very deep, miniature five-panel face and carved ivory pull.

"*Gadabout* has a legend?"

"Oh yes."

She puts the drawer back and opens another. Max likes telling the story.

"The boat was built to help seven sailors find their way home."

Rebecca is looking inside.

"It's written into the bill of sale. Ownership can't transfer until the previous owner's drawer has been filled. The Estate has to approve."

"The Estate?"

"The builder was quite formal, an old New Bedford whaling family."

She opens the first of the drawers again. Above is a set of shelves, Max's personal library. Across the stern are more lockers and shelves, everything raised wood panels, everything deep, dark cherry. Along the port side the big double bunk sits over a pair of captain's drawers. At the foot of the bed a bulkhead returns with an arched door to the private head. The head has a full size tub. Rebecca likes taking baths. A skylight, similar to those out in the salon, lets the stars down into the cabin.

She reaches into the drawer and pulls out a green plastic ring: it's set with a cheap silver shamrock, the toy you might find in a Cracker Jacks box. She tries slipping it onto her finger, too small. She pouts and Max shrugs.

"A hundred possibilities there."

She puts the ring back into the drawer.

The next contains an old black and white photo, a family standing in front of a tenement, light gray stars pinned to their dark woolen coats. Max knows the inscription, *Warsaw, '38, DaDa and Pops, Mom 2nd from left*. Rebecca's eyes tear up. Though she's told him she's Roman Catholic he suspects from other things she has said, the shape of her face, those Mediterranean eyes, her grandparents emigrating from Europe around that time. Maybe they chose the church for protection, who could blame them in those days? She touches the face of the photo, looks over, attempting a smile, then slips it back into the drawer.

Contained in the third is a folded note, tattered and torn, bleeding ink as though it might have got wet.

"Sorry it took me so long. I miss you," Max says.

Rebecca reaches inside.

"Be careful, it's practically dust."

The note is like tissue paper, as if the owner carried it many years. When Max touched it that first day the folds fell apart. She decides not to touch it, closing the drawer, gently.

She goes to open the fourth. Max can't wait. Rebecca catches her breath, everyone does, she sees what's inside and brings a hand to her heart. He's wondering how the earrings look in the lamplight, how the rubies shine in their silver settings.

"Are those … ?"

"You better believe it," Max says.

There's also a watch, a Breitling, the Mariner's model. In *Gadabout's* letter of sale there are instructions for the watch and earrings to be polished every six months. For the first two years that Max owned the boat the estate actually sent a man out to check, an attorney no less. One time he flew to New Zealand. Now they send an affidavit for Max to sign, notarized of course.

"You can't try them on," Max says, knowing that's what she's thinking. "They've never been worn."

Rebecca purses her lips, slowly closing the drawer, turning back into the light, lifting her hair with both hands and exposing the length of her neck, his second most favorite spot. Then she goes back to the drawers.

"It's empty?" she says, holding the next.

"I'm the fifth owner."

They're getting dangerously close. He imagines he's carved a note in the bottom, *I had cancer.* She's shaking it just to be sure.

"I guess I'm still not home," Max says.

Rebecca places the drawer back in its slot, walks to where he is sitting there on the bunk.

"I am," she says, pushing him back against the pile of pillows, taking his cock into her mouth. It's been like that all day – gently, or not so gently – whatever they're feeling that moment. Max runs his hand up the back of her neck, her hair luxuriously tight in his grasp.

"Becca," he says.

She buries her face up against him, pressing, gagging, the same desperation he feels whenever he gets inside her, like he'll never get far enough. Pulling her back, pushing her down on the bunk, he lifts her legs and enters in one, deep thrust.

"Max," she moans, "My Max."

They're both coming. Max is afraid he might crush her but she doesn't mind, holding him tight with legs clamped hard at his neck. They both explode. He's lost again in the sound of her voice; she's there in that other dimension, their bodies melting toward sleep.

"Don't ever leave me," she whispers, her face beside his there on the pillow, "Tell me you'll stay forever."

Conflict

by Gloria Garfunkel

Well, Mixed Mood Episode Ralph and Chloe are having lots of stupid fights over trivia and nearly broke up. We can never remember what the fights are about. Everything bugs me. She moved out for three days until we met for dinner tonight and made up while the Episode was diminishing. She understands it was the bipolar. Her father was like that most of the time. We went to a double-feature zombie movie which cheered us both up, especially *The Night of the Living Dead*, which is exactly how I feel when I'm depressed.

I'd had a really bad day at work. I got into conflicts with about ten annoying people. Serena, the Borderline Secretary pointed out thirteen of my errors to Stan Stealth, my Sociopathic boss and so he had a fit, jumping on his chair while I sat next to it pretending to be intimidated. Serena is one of those compulsive cat hoarders who lives with 27 felines in a decrepit mansion she inherited from her parents. Meanwhile, I tried to get my assistant, Passive-Aggressive Al, to help me and he said yes to everything as usual and then surfed the Internet all day. At least Chloe and I are getting along now.

For April Fool's this year this numbskull in our department who thinks he's a genius sent around a phony memo from Orwellian Headquarters that the whole

33

psychiatry department is being laid off due to lack of business. I freaked out and started contemplating suicide. I though of jumping from Orwellian's thirteenth floor (the roof) though on the elevator up I hear it's an April Fool's joke. I wanted to strangle Irving, but I'm still in Mixed territory and have to control my emotions. I have no idea what I'll be like at the family Seder on April 14 that Chloe really wants to go to. My whole toxic Jewish tribe sets me off, sitting at a chanting meal until 2 AM. I may claim a migraine or just take a few extra Zyprexa and Valium which, with the four cups of ritual wine, should do the trick.

After the movie tonight Chloe asked if I thought my family was as bad as the zombies. I said they are worse because they are all Holocaust survivors and the six million are more present than the real live people. It gets kind of crowded.

Rose

by John Wentworth Chapin

"I think I might be done for the day," Charles says, flexing cramped fingers. Black spots appear in his vision from screen strain.

Esther grunts disagreement. Charles gets a charge from this; when he first visited Esther, he feared he wore thin her patience, but now – if he reads her clearly – she wants him around. The laptop glow lights their wearying faces. *Astral projection, past lives, transient ischemic attack, telekinesis, psychotic break, demonic possession* – such an exhausting mishmash of fact and crap. They have watched videos about Xtreme sports and the Hoover Dam and faith healers and read about Alistair Crowley and extinct big cats, all while listening to a Pandora Motown playlist.

She reclines in a rental hospital bed in her dining room; Charles sits next to her in a plastic chair, leaning forward. The laptop rests on Esther's abdomen, her dry forefinger resting on the trackpad while Charles cradles the wireless keyboard on his lap. She clicks, he types.

Their research agenda has reached something of a dead end. Esther mowed down several pedestrians late last year, killing three, and Charles, witnessing it, narrowly avoided a similar fate. She's trying to understand how she could have done such a thing; Charles, his own agenda tied to hers, is trying to find where to go next. This was clearly The Big

Wake-Up Call, but now he's climbing down a ladder, reaching his foot backwards and downwards for the next rung and finding no secure place to step.

"It blows my mind how much people've put right on the Internet," Esther says, scrolling through Google search results. "When I retired from the library, card catalogs were already a thing of the past. But ... it was nothing like this."

"The whole world," Charles nods.

Esther sucks on her teeth, the pink tip of her tongue protruding between her parched lips. "And most of it isn't worth a second of thought," she says. "People write poems, put them out there. Governments put all sorts of data out there. Who reads it all? Phone bills. People's family pictures. *Blogs*." Esther showed brief interest in blogs a few weeks ago until she was put off by *knotty sentences*: as far as Charles could tell, these were convoluted or grammatically transgressive or both.

Esther stares up at the ceiling, silent long enough that Charles glances at her.

"You okay?" he asks.

She laughs to herself and Charles waits.

"I am 74 years old, and do you know what? I have never seen pornography."

Charles freezes: not what he was expecting.

Esther says, "You've seen pornography? Of course you have."

"Well, I mean, everyone has ... I mean most people my age."

"Good. Let's watch a pornography movie."

Charles lets out a loud, strange sound, something between a cough and a laugh and a yelp, something he can only think of as *explurting*.

"There's no call to be embarrassed," she says. "I have no intention of being titillated. Or maybe I will be. Who knows? I'm an old woman and I should be able to watch a pornography if everyone else does."

Charles laughs without humor, his throat dry.

"You'll get over it," she says. "Just take me to a pornography site you've been to before."

"Wow. This is totally ... Okay. I guess you put me on the spot. You know I'm gay, right?" he asks.

"No, I didn't."

"Really?"

"Well, I didn't *know it* until you just now told me. You can put on something gay if you would prefer."

"I would most definitely not prefer!" Charles explurts. "Tell me what to type and I'll type it."

"*Sex movie*," she says. He types it in. They scroll the results: no porn. She tries a few others: *pornography, dirty movie*. Nothing.

He smirks when she offers *smut*, and she glares. "You know you could find it in a heartbeat, but instead of helping me, you get childish."

"This embarrasses me," Charles says. "Try something more specific. Something ... dirty."

"Pussy," she spits out.

Charles gasps for air and then types and hits ENTER. Esther scrolls, pausing at THE VICE GUIDE TO EATING PUSSY, but then to his relief she moves down the list. Nothing.

She frowns at him and reclines, arms crossed. "You won't help?"

Next to *pussy*, he types *video fucking* and hits ENTER. Esther grunts a laugh; he wishes he had left SafeSearch on, but it's too late. "This is totally humiliating," he says.

"You will survive," Esther reminds him as she clicks and a bright pink screen comes up with thumbnail images promising a cornucopia of smut. Esther leans forward, carefully examining the images. Charles looks away, but he can hear. Click. Grunt. Click. *Ohmygodohmygod*. Click. Squeal. Click. Dance music. Click. *Yeahyeahyeahyeah*. Click. Gasp. Click. *Fuck yeah*.

37

Esther's silence is excruciating, and when he finally looks at her face to catch her reaction, he catches nothing.

The pornathon lasts about twenty minutes. When Charles returns from the bathroom, she has closed the laptop.

"When can you come back over here?" she asks.

Charles is silent. He was thinking in the bathroom, taking his time.

"I won't make you type *pussy* again, if that's what you're worried about," she says.

"Ha. Ha. Ha. I'm going home to take a shower and pretend this never happened."

"But you are coming back."

"I'm not sure of my schedule. Ever since my disastrous Indian meditation retreat – well, longer, really – I have been thinking about quitting my job."

"To do what?" she asks.

"I don't know. Something *more*."

"Don't quit your job without a plan. That's a mistake. Instead of pulling back from work, step toward it."

"You had a *career*. I have a *job*. I don't know what I want! I tried dating. I tried painting. I have been reading. I tried meditation and travel and I don't know what else to try." Charles hears the shabbiness of his argument, and that makes it all the worse.

"And what does that have to do with earning a living?" Esther sighs. "When you get ice cream, they let you try every flavor on a little plastic spoon if you want. You act like you've tasted them all and then ordered vanilla, still complaining because you wanted something different."

This sits between then for a moment, Charles struggling with it and Esther satisfied.

He says, "I'm supposed to choose between twelve flavors someone else has picked? How limited is that?"

38

She nods. "And you think the problem is that you don't have enough time to find out different things?"

"It's four months since the accident," he says. "I've been floating ever since. I want to feel grounded."

"You are assuming there's something you can find that will make it all better. Maybe it's *you* you need to fix, not your routine."

Charles winces, hearing her name his unrelenting fear: the accident left his body unscathed but damaged his mind.

They are silent. She quietly moves her finger on the edge of the laptop's aluminum casing, now coral pink in the evening light. They are both silent for a long moment.

Esther says, "The last few times you've come ... Well, I can't walk and they tell me I never will. I got big worries about lawsuits." She'd mentioned before the lawsuits – three accident victims' families seeking damages, insurance companies – but not the worry. "I can't go through all that. It's time for me to go, and I want your help."

Charles takes a moment to register what she's asking, and when he looks at her, she stares back with moist, resigned eyes.

"You don't mean *that*," he says.

"But I do."

"Now?"

"No, not now. But ... soon."

He wants to say something clever, to undo what she has just asked, but she's clear and lucid and her chin is set: there's no arguing. He falters, "The porn – ?"

She smiles at him. "Not my final request, just curiosity."

Another silence lingers, this time each searching in the pale pink glow for the truth in the other's eyes.

"You haven't answered me," Esther murmurs.

Charles doesn't give an answer because he doesn't have one.

Kiss Off

by Lynn Beighley

Bill Plover eats slowly. He chews each bite many, many, many, many, many times. 32 times, to be precise. I know this because I've been counting.

"Have you ever heard of Fletcherizing?" Bill asked me what seems like three hours ago. "Nature will castigate those who don't masticate." I've figured out that when Bill asks me a question, he isn't actually asking. When he asks, "do you know xyz?" he really means, "let me tell you all about xyz in excruciating detail."

Horace Fletcher had theories about eating, things like the importance of chewing each bite of food 32 times, and chewing about 100 times per minute. I know lots more about Horace Fletcher's theories about eating. Look him up if you're curious. I'm going to try to forget.

I'm on a date with Bill Plover. America set me up. A week ago, Bill came in to the office, complete with camera crew, and very expensive chocolates. (I later discovered the candy was from a sponsor. Bill told me. He didn't have to tell me, but of course he did, because that's what Bill Plover does.)

"Hello, Jenn, these are for you." I looked up. Some guy awkwardly handed me a huge gift-wrapped box. No, not some guy, it was Bill. He didn't look like Bill. No god-awful free t-shirt from a software vendor covered in stains, no baggy sweatpants, no grungy sneakers. Instead, he was in slacks and a button-up-the-front grown-up shirt. His heavy stegosaurus body was gone, and in its place was a good-looking, if slightly stocky man. It wasn't quite on the level of an Eliza Dolittle transformation, but it wasn't that far off.

And shit, I was the one who looked terrible. I was the one in a stained t-shirt, courtesy of a loose lid on my coffee cup. And ragged jeans. And flip-flops, for godsake.

"Jenn, America has spoken. Will you do me the great honor of accompanying me to dinner next Friday?"

Of course I wouldn't. I mean, despite the window dressing, this was Bill Plover, a man I don't like. A man I most certainly don't want to date.

"Yes," I said. Why didn't I say no? I meant to say no, but did I say no?

No, I said yes. I said yes because he paused before and faltered after he said the words "will you." Because he looked at me like my cat Pollock does when I open a can of cat food. I said yes because this was important to him, and hell, it was just one date. One date. It might even be fun, I thought. I thought this because I'm stupid.

There's a bored-looking guy with a camera at the next table. I look at him and he smiles at me, gives me a thumbs up. Maybe I can get his number.

It should come as no surprise that we're at an all-you-can-eat-gosh-darn-buffet. And Bill is chewing. And chewing. Also chewing. I watch his mouth move, I think about his teeth and his tongue behind his lips. I have been focused on his mouth all night.

Bill stops chewing. He swallows. Then he takes another bite. Bill Plover continues to plow through the courses he must finish to accomplish his meticulously thought out plan to get the most out of this meal, even if he's not paying for it. I finished some time ago. And so I find myself staring at his mouth, wondering what it will be like to kiss him. Because I might have to kiss him goodnight. I mean,

41

America expects it, right? Oh, but wait, this is Bill. He's not going to kiss me. We'll shake hands. Yes. That will be it. I relax.

"You filled up on the bread, that's where you went wrong," Bill says. He smiles and I notice a bit of spinach on his front tooth. I don't tell him. I say nothing, even though a tiny voice from an earpiece in my right ear tells me to say, "I'd rather fill up on you." What is wrong with this woman?

You lovely viewers at home won't know this, but I've got a little earpiece on and some producer lady on the other end is trying to tell me what to say. She keeps trying to get me to flirt with Bill. Possibly it's for comic relief for the audience, because I suspect Bill wouldn't know flirting if it bit him in the ass. Or something. I'm not going to test that theory.

We're finally, somehow, at the end. It's over. Well, almost over. He's walked me to my car, the cameraman sticking close by.

"I had a very nice time tonight, Jenn." He smiles, and the spinach is gone. He leans in and what the hell, I kiss him. And it's warm, and his lips are soft, and I like it. He's good at this. He touches my face, and I can't think anymore.

And then it's over, and I can't speak and I'm alone. Except for the voice in my ear that whispers, "wow."

My Bunny

by Andrew Stancek

I've allowed the travesty and can't forgive myself.

My heart is breaking. Oh, not like pop songs on the radio about the boyfriend stolen by a best friend, nothing like that. My heart overflows; that's how it's broken. I never knew a small body could produce so many tears. I cannot dry out.

Everybody snatches a piece of my baby. They compare him to inventors, scientists, mystics, Einstein, Pauling, Linnaeus, saints even, throw around names I've never heard and don't want to.

I believe, you know. Fine, laugh. A reasonably educated woman in the twenty-first century says, with a straight face, "I believe". I'm not talking about fire and brimstone although there's plenty of good even in that, and we'd be better off with a little lava instead of online porn and music videos, no limits on anything, no morality or wonder and when I get going like this they laugh and say, "Yveta, slow down," but I can't slow down, my heart wells up and the water bursts the surface and I cry and I pray and I know what I know. I am right and they are wrong and I don't care who they are and what degrees they have or what TV show they've appeared on; it makes me so agitated and he's still my little bunny I want back and I wish none of it had ever happened.

He's a freak. The first time I saw him called that on the cover of one of those supermarket rags, I dropped the jar of spaghetti sauce I was holding and made a huge mess. What do you mean, freak? He's my boy, who's come up with a glorious way to help everybody, and where do they get off calling him names? I thought people like Beyoncé, or movie stars, or that Aniston woman from *Friends*, that they choose fame, and they deserve the tabloids, but my little one, he did not have any choice.

He was so sick, a sweet little sick boy, underweight and born five weeks premature and had to be in an incubator, and even when he was with me, he cuddled and gurgled and had those curls and eyelashes, and every mother is crazy about her little boy, the precious gift that came out of her and I just loved him to death. But I didn't. It's a stupid phrase, isn't it? When I get excited my voice goes really really high and my hands flutter and I flush and I catch myself and hear what I've said and I wonder, "What did I just say? Where did that come from?" And I cry.

I already said that, didn't I? Well, it's still true.

I wish I was dead sometimes. I even wish he was dead, or I'd never had him. Those are sins; I know that. I've talked to Father Czestochowa a lot. He's helped. He says I have an overwrought sense of sin, that I'm too concerned about understanding and blame. "Accept. Give it over to Jesus and to Our Lady," he says. I try. They say God will never give you a bigger burden than you can carry, never. But it's always people who have suffered little who say that. How can they know? There I go again. I know nothing about other people and their suffering. Who am I to say?

I sure know my own burdens, my own cross. My Adam, my little Bunny, he's my cross. I don't blame my husband for leaving. Sometimes I think he was right to do it. I was bitter but I understood then and I understand better now. I had no time for him and knew I never would. Adam was a part of me, my flesh and blood and Frank, well, he was just a husband, just a man. He stopped being important the minute Adam took sick.

I've read every book which deals with Perthes disease. At the university library they got me articles and studies and translations from all kinds of languages, some you wouldn't think would know anything about medicine at all, but there I go shooting off my mouth again before I've thought. The point is I wanted to understand. My sister pulled at her ear and grimaced when I started talking about the latest research, or a study conducted in Malaysia and promising results at the clinic in Caracas. "Yveta," she said. "You need another interest. Maybe I'll get you a puppy. You liked dogs when you were little. Would you like a little Pomeranian?" So I had to watch myself and pretend I was fine. I was fine. I was obsessive, I know I was, but that doesn't mean I wasn't fine. I knew that disease inside out and then some.

Adam, he was obsessive, too. Sure I know where that comes from. Is it in the genes, I wonder, or a quirk? He read a lot about genes, too, but not this part. He says humans used to have a flying gene, which over the millennia bred out, more and more recessive. I don't know if he's making that up or some scientist really wrote a study.

I don't want to give him over to the world. I don't want him to be famous, have his face all over every magazine. I told Father Czestochowa that I am sure it's a terrible sin to want your child to be different. But most mothers, when they think that, they want their sons to be more special. I want mine to be ordinary, to stock shelves in a grocery store, play hockey with buddies, drink beer, get into trouble. My Adam will never have any of that. He's like John Lennon or Elvis. What I have to look forward to is Graceland.

I don't know if I can forgive myself, ever.

Better Bring an Umbrella

by Rachel Ambrose

Whatever they might say about showers in April, it can't compare to the maelstrom of April that I'm having. Just in this first week alone, Blake has whisked me off to Tamarind Heights (the hip young town two towns away) for a long weekend. We stayed in a gorgeous hotel I wanted to wrap up and put in my pocket, drank fancy cocktails with swizzle sticks and fruit twists, and have had more sex than I thought possible to have in one weekend. The reason? He's sold a rather fabulous painting for a rather fabulous price, and we decided to celebrate. We laugh together more than I've ever laughed with anyone; everything is hilarious for absolutely no reason and his eyes are the most beautiful green lanterns I've ever seen.

Things aren't so rosy with other aspects of my life, though. My meager pay is having a lot of trouble standing up to the fine dining that Blake loves. Even when we stay in, I spend premium money on starfruit (his favorite), arborio rice, and organic meats. He chips in by bringing along lovely bottles of wine, but I always wake up expecting my bank account to be flatter than my hair. And my relationship with Charlotte and Isa, my housemate and ex-housemate respectively, has been suffering too. Charlotte was furious after she discovered my theft of her wine, and refused to speak to me for three days. I canceled plans with

Isa last week in order to spend more time with Blake. I knew that it was a bad idea when I first thought of it, but like all bad ideas, it stayed in my ear, whispering its simpering little sentences until I agreed to it. But I can't help bad behavior; I'm in love and I don't have to account to anyone except myself and Blake. I'm practically entitled to it! Who else matters? It's me and him against the world for all I care. Isn't that what all the books and movies have taught me?

I'm learning, much to my dismay, that the sunlit glow I expected the world to take on, transferred magically from all the movies I've seen, doesn't really exist, which is rude. It should.

When I was little, my biggest fantasy was dancing around in a beautiful dress to Frank Sinatra while a gorgeous guy clasped my hands and spun me so fast my head would spin. It never occurred to me that there would be real life tied up in all that. I'm in love! What do you mean I still have to pay my bills on time?

To make up for the world's utter lack of whimsy, today I've tied my hair up in little knots and dusted my face with cinnamon rouge, and taken myself to work humming a Dvorak sonatina. Just because I have to work in a charmless office doesn't mean I have to take it as drudgery. Mrs. Hatfield is in court today, wonder of wonders, so I type in blissful silence, composing love letters to Blake in my head as I lick and stamp envelopes, imagining covering his body in sultry kisses as I dust Mrs. Hatfield's desk. It really does help my grumpiness at the world refusing to transform into sunshine and daisies. After work, congratulating myself on my magnanimity, I call Isa.

"Hi honey!" I chirrup into the phone when she picks up. "How about a girls' night out tonight, just me and you? We can go to that new South African place you've been talking about!"

"Oh," she says, and I can hear the hesitation in her

47

voice. "Um, sure, that sounds good. Is Blake coming?"

"No, silly goose!" I reply, laughing. "He's not a girl, is he? Besides, we need some time apart from each other, I need to feel like my hand isn't being constantly held."

"Sounds like a nice problem to have," she says, sighing. "But fine, I'll meet you at the Peri-Peri Cafe at six, sound good?"

"Sure!" I say breezily. I go home, change clothes and run a brush through my hair, showing up at the restaurant a few minutes to six. I grab a table and look up in relief as the door swing open and Isa walks in.

"Hello friend!" I call to her fondly. She swings her bag down and plants herself in a chair, running a hand through her hair, looking inexplicably grumpy. Am I seriously the only happy person in the world? I wonder.

"What's up in your corner of the world?" I ask as the waitress brings us glasses of water and menus. "I feel like we haven't seen each other in ages."

"That's because we haven't," points out Isa, and I clue in that that's probably why she's less than blissed out.

"Well, you're here now!" I say brightly. "And looking rather gorgeous in a very windswept way if I do say so myself!"

Isa sips her water and smiles coldly at me. "Don't try to butter me up. I'm really mad at you."

"Why?" I ask, scrunching up my face and tilting my head. "Because of Blake?"

"Because you managed to steal Blake right out from under Charlotte's nose!" says Isa, and I try not to wince, because there's a part of me who thinks she might be right about that. "She was set to ask him out at his birthday party, and then you came in and formed this magical connection with him, and –"

"Hang on," I interrupt her. "She knew him way before I did, she could have formed a magical connection with him any time she wanted. But he liked me, so he asked me out, and now we're dating, and she missed her chance. That's all." I lightly slap my hand against the table before crossing my arms defiantly across my chest.

"Well, you don't have to parade him around in her face all the time," Isa says. "Talking about all your dates and plans and what dresses to wear."

I roll my eyes. "God forbid she be happy for me. Or you be happy for me, for that matter."

"You both are my friends!" she protests. "You can have him, just don't be an asshole about it. And call me more. It's not easy taking care of my brother when I have basically no help," she continues, and I see how tired she is; her eyes are bloodshot, and her skin is in serious need of some exfoliation.

"I'm sorry," I say, reaching across the table to pat her hand. "I promise I'll be a better friend. Do you want me to cook for you or anything?"

"Please," Isa says, cracking her first real smile as the waitress comes over to take our order. "We both know you don't know how to boil water, honey. But it's okay, I love you anyway."

Two in the Hand are Worth One in the Bush

by Gill Hoffs

Today it's Neil and a working dinner with Russian clients who expect me to nod in the right places, smile constantly, and not mind if they pat my bottom or slide a hand between my thighs – or so I presume from similar dinners with Neil's visitors in the same upmarket club. Neil is nice enough though somewhat windy, with a small cock and a big portfolio. Working with him has led to other business opportunities for me, as well as the occasional loan of a Porsche, so I don't mind smiling 'til my cheeks ache and sitting in a booth with my legs apart under the tablecloth while strangers check for tampons or coils or whatever it is they're doing in there. If it feels like they might catch their Rolex in my pubic hair or I suspect they could do with a manicure – or worse, they've been eating spicy finger food – I clench my cunt muscles like I need to hold in a litre of pee, and wriggle so they think I'm just tight and enjoying myself.

No knickers necessary. Stockings a must. Apart from that, I know Neil prefers little black dresses with low backs and fronts, for me to wear my hair up in a chignon so he can let it down later as he humps me from behind, and red lips and nails. He's collecting me from the agency – I don't yet trust him with my home address – at 4pm for coffee and a chat about who's who before we meet the Russians at 5. I've taken some Clarityn in case he turns up with any of the flowers I'm allergic to (sneezes can lead to all sorts of injuries during a blowjob), refreshed my admittedly basic knowledge of Russian, and have ten minutes to listen to the Beastie Boys before my taxi honks a welcome outside my window. When it comes I grab my overnight clutch (condoms, makeup, mints, toothbrush) and off I go.

The Russians have brought their own hostesses to the club, no one I know, girls with badly-bleached hair and animal print dresses and Blackpool accents. Neil keeps glancing from them to me, and I can guess what's running through his mind: that the Russians he is so keen to impress think him a fool to have brought me, that I'm too posh, that they might choose to broker their deals with one of his co-workers instead. He warned me of this once, when we first met.

"The men I do business with sometimes judge a man's balls by the women he empties them into. I trust you will not let me down."

I'd nodded. I understood. So now, when he introduces me formally to his guests, I slip my arm round his waist for a reassuring squeeze, then make a point of sitting myself between the most important Russians of the group, sliding along the leather seating in the 'U'-shaped booth and allowing my dress to ride up as I move into place. When the man to my left glances down, he cannot fail to notice the tops of my stockings, trimmed with tacky red lace, and the suspenders dividing my creamy thighs into inner and outer segments just begging to be touched. I smile at Neil, off to the right, and open my legs a little while my hands fuss with the white linen napkin provided for me on the table. Once

51

the Russian has seen what I've got to offer, I can drape it loosely over my lap. The other women are fiddling with chunky bracelets, checking the state of their stick-on nails, and waiting for their vodkas to arrive. Neil sees where my neighbours are looking and flashes me a tiny wink.

Drinks arrive, then food, and while the Russians talk figures and schedules with Neil, and the girls knock back their drinks and giggle, the man on my left eases his hand over my thigh and into my crotch, my napkin hiding his hand from my other neighbour's sight. Neil has a lot riding on this dinner, a contract for 2,000 forklift trucks and operative training or something similar, and I don't want to let him down or miss out on a bonus that could mean a conservatory for my mum. So while my right hand uses a silver fork to rearrange the salad on my plate, and my head nods along with their conversation out of polite interest, my left hand tugs the hem of my dress higher then slides into the Russian's lap. Just a semi? Feeling somewhat aggrieved, I knead and allow myself to be groped until there's a satisfyingly hard cock bulging beneath his smart black trousers. I squirm against his signet ring, fork a bit of rocket into my mouth, and murmur "Mmmm …" near his ear. I hope the man on my other side doesn't try anything until his boss is done with me.

"Your deal sounds … too expensive to me. You understand, I need a profit too, da?"

Neil stares at his drink for a moment, swirling it in his glass, before replying.

"Of course. But in the current climate …" he raises his shoulders and drops them again. "I want to give you the best deal possible, for you are not just my fellow businessmen, but my friends." The Russian's hand stills between my legs. "But there is only so much I can take off the price, you understand, before I am paying for the trucks and expertise myself."

I drop my fork under the table. It takes some doing, as I have to pretend to knock it from my lap onto the floor by mistake, but the Russian moves his hand and allows me to slip underneath to retrieve it. The tablecloth drapes down enough to give the space under the large round table a tent-like Bedouin feel, but I'm the only woman in this particular harem.

I love being ambidextrous, I think it gives me a certain edge at these business dinners, especially when two of my client's clients need distracting at once. Two zips are eased down at once, two cocks freed from tight underwear, one hard, one hardening. I check for cheese, spit on one, and rub it clean as sensually as I can, then wipe my hand on the carpet. Bobbing my head between them both, sucking the heads, swirling my tongue, and wanking them hard, I mentally doff my cap at the one who wasn't pawing my crotch a minute ago for not so much as flinching as I reached for his cock.

Unsurprisingly, the fingerfucker cums first, grabbing my head under the table while he spunks at my tonsils. I suck him clean, swallow, then finish off his co-worker with a tickle of the balls. Grabbing my fork from the floor, I slip up into my seat as gracefully as I can, sip vodka to rinse the taste from my mouth, then smile at Neil. He looks a lot happier, sitting back in his seat instead of leaning towards the other businessmen, and I'm pleased. I'm also glad to see the lights have dimmed near our table.

I check my reflection using the back of a knife. I'm glad the lip-sealant that gives my food such a bitter aftertaste has done its job while my mouth was working on suckjobs. A waiter brings a tray of coffee and mints, and I discreetly palm three of the strong white sweets. I'm looking forward to going back to Neil's hotel room for a nice long soak. He *always* books a suite with a Jacuzzi. I suspect it's to conceal his farts from whoever is sharing the tub.

Then I feel hands on my thighs again. Hands. Plural. I ease my legs as far apart as I can, so my knees are hard against my neighbours' legs, in the vain hope that their hands won't meet somewhere in the middle. I don't want any conflict near my crotch. Resting my head on my hand, I dangle a napkin from my palm as if I've forgotten I'm holding it in the vodka fog now lingering around our booth, and lean my elbow on the table. I try and look like I'm concentrating on what Neil is saying to the Russian on the far left while I clasp the most senior Russian, my neighbour on the left, by the hand and guide it to my boob, then pull my dress down below the nipple. For whatever reason, guys don't feel like they're handling enough of your tit until they touch nipple. The way I'm holding my arm, my bare breast is unlikely to be seen.

When Neil raises his index finger for the bill, the Russians withdraw their hands, leaving me free to rearrange my chest and hemline. We scoot round the table, stand up, and say our goodbyes, and I pop a couple of mints in my mouth before Neil takes my arm and leads me out to the street.

"Whatever you did to them, it was bloody brilliant – I closed the deal!"

He moves in to kiss me. I put a finger on his lips and smile.

"Menthol makes you tingle. I want to celebrate with you and suck you dry … just let me crunch this mint first."

Not spring not winter

by Susan Tepper

Plans must be revised. Schools changed. I light a cigarette and sit back in my barcalounger. Some woman I once tried to fuck sat there after things didn't work out. She sat there naked. Her breasts hung like half-filled feed bags for a horse. After she left, I sniffed the fake leather seat but it still didn't get me off.

Twice this week I noticed a person in a uniform looking toward my car as I drove up to the fenced part, where the shrubbery is thickest. The fence that separates the little kiddies, my little darlings, from me and the rest of the world. I don't give a fuck about the rest of the world. Let's be clear on that. But the damned motherfucker in uniform had this laser vision that I swear could pop holes in the side of my car. I just kept going. It's been a few days. No little darlings to watch at their play on the jungle gym or tossing balls to each other. Those sweet hands reaching, reaching, grasping the ball.

Swoon the white rat sits on my lap. I finger his genitals. Genitalia. A lilting word. Italian in origin? *Genitaliaaaaaaaaaaa* I sing out like an opera star. Then decide to cruise the school yard at California Avenue. It's almost lunch time, time for recess. I stamp out the cigarette in a Las Vegas ashtray; a showgirl type with good, full boobs glazed into the bottom.

At California Avenue if all looks safe I will stop the car. It's a good name. There should be palm trees.

I get into my black windbreaker. Putting Swoon in the windbreaker pocket, I head out. The day is blustery – not spring not winter. I am this weather. Nothing. It occurs to me staring up at the grey sky. Neither man nor beast is who am I. Swoon wiggling my pocket. I have this urge to squeeze his neck till it runs dry.

Fevered

by Jessica McHugh

Edward McKenzie blows his nose on the last tissue and grumbles at his reflection. His pallid face and bright red nose make him look like a clown – or his mother Betty on a bender.

Closing his eyes, he pats his nose with the powder puff. Even his brain-thumping congestion can't sever what the scent conjures. He breathes in, and Eleanor sits beside him. With a smile, she takes the powder puff and hands him a bowl of chicken noodle soup.

Get better first, dear. There's no one here to impress.

Edward groans. "Thanks for reminding me."

He cinches his robe and pulls off his wig, but the hair snags on his crucifix. Tearing it free, he breaks the chain, and the crucifix falls into the Duska powder on the dressing table. Sighing, he plucks it out and sets it aside.

"I'm sorry, Grandma. You're not to blame for my problems."

Darling, your problems only grow as big you allow – the more you nourish them, the stronger they get. Be a bad gardener for once.

She tweaks his raw nose and grabs the spoon. Ladling broth into his mouth, she warms him with more than soup.

When the phone rings, the spoon falls, clanging on the dressing table. He flinches at the sound: Edward doesn't receive many calls. Pressing the receiver to his ear, he squeaks. "Hello?"

"Hello. May I speak to Father Edward McKenzie, please?"

"This is he."

"Oh, Edward, I didn't recognize your voice. It's Father Timothy Ballard."

He sniffles. "I have a cold," he says. "What can I do for you, Timothy?"

"This won't take long. I just wanted to ask if you were interested in filling Father Sheridan's spot at St. Anthony's this summer?" Father Ballard says. "It's a summer health studies class with approximately thirteen eighth graders. It should only last a month at most." After a silence, he clears his throat and continues. "If you're not comfortable, I understand. I just thought you might enjoy a change of scenery. You've seemed a little down lately."

Edward holds his breath. Except for Eleanor, he assumes most people don't notice his emotions.

"The position wouldn't begin until June. Are you interested?"

Edward looks over to see Grandma Eleanor nod. *This could be what you've been waiting for.*

His mind whirs, the words jumbled. But his answer tumbles out in a powerful, "Yes, I'll *do* it!"

"Excellent. You're really helping us out of a jam."

Father Timothy says goodbye, but Edward doesn't hang up. A voice speaks to him from the other end. His mother's biting words tell him to call Timothy back and refuse the position.

"Children, Edward. You and children. If you can't see the trouble there, you're sicker than I thought," she says.

His vision fogs with fever. Standing in a corner, Betty taps her cane. "A thing like you shouldn't be around kids. And a health class? What does a cross-dressing freak like you know about being healthy?"

"I would never do anything to hurt a child."

"Not intentionally, but your perversion could spread just the same. What if a child asks about homosexuality? Would you advise him to pursue that life?"

His throat is dry, and it hurts to swallow. "I will teach the curriculum," he says. Betty scoffs, swinging her cane as she strides toward him. He collapses back onto the couch, sweat pouring down his face.

"You'll lie," she says. "Lie, lie, lie – that's all you do, Edward. From your secret desires to your insane visions." He squints at her, and she snickers. "What, you didn't think I knew about Eleanor? How you see her, how you speak to her?"

He screams "Stop!" but Betty steps closer, her cane moving up his leg. It flips up his robe, exposing his garters.

He covers his legs and stands, the fever spinning his vision. He stumbles, knocking against the dressing table. The soup spills, and the bowl breaks on the floor.

Edward wheezes in torment, bent over the mess. The hand on his back comforts, so he knows it can't be his mother's.

Ssh … It's okay, Edward, calm down.

Lifting his head, cold sweat runs off his chin. His mother is gone. The pain subsides.

"Eleanor …"

Yes, I'm here.

"I don't know what I'm going to do. I took a teaching position – I agreed to – oh God Almighty, I'm so confused."

She pats his hair. *The fever's breaking, dear. You'll be all right.*

Gasping at the mess on the floor, she crouches to clean it. Edward stops her, holds her hands, and whispers, "I think I made the biggest mistake of my life."

She touches her hand to his cheek and smiles.

Oh Edward. If a man spends his life trying not to make mistakes and remains unhappy, perhaps allowing a mistake is the first and greatest step to joy.

All Greased Up, Nowhere to Go

by Shane Simmons

Stood outside the Chinese buffet restaurant, I wait alone. Inside, it's already packed. Through the steamed-up windows I watch them, gathered around melamine tables, gorging upon mountainous plate-loads, forks shovelling mounds of grease into open gobs.

I shudder.

A man, at least three times my size, walks out of the door and brings with him the inviting smells of chow mein, roast pork and five spice. I haven't eaten since breakfast, and my stomach rumbles. Then I turn my nose up when the enticement is lost in the haze of the big man's cigarette smoke.

The mobile in my hand beeps.

"See you soon!!!!!!!!!!!!" I roll my eyes and hit 'delete'. Having already been kept waiting a good half-hour, I tap my feet wondering just what 'soon' means in Sandra's world.

She wants my opinion on her new bloke; not that my opinion has ever counted for shit before. This is the one night we all happen to be free. Must remember not to call him Stephen. Stephen – "That Bastard" – was the previous one, but I'm sure it won't be long until this one becomes an honorary bastard too. I feel a tad guilty for writing off the guy before I've set eyes on him, but in Sandra's life, history is always playing on repeat.

Farther down the road I spot her marching up, one hand waving cobwebs out of the sky, her other arm entwined with the companion she's marching beside.

"Sorry we're late, we got, 'erm' ... delayed!" She winks as she disentangles herself from her companion and leaning in, gives me a peck on the cheek. I cringe as I try to bleach the image she's conjured from my mind.

"This is Marlon! I've told him ALL about you!"

I offer my hand to him but it hangs mid-air, waiting, as he plays away with his mobile. Eventually, with his eyes still glued to his phone, his hand brushes past my own and it feels more like a tickle than a firm, hetero handshake.

"I trust it was all positive." I know Sandra has a habit of revealing the little dirt she has on me to all and sundry.

"When it comes to you, what good is there to say?"

She drags her man through the glass doors of the restaurant. Under my breath I whisper, "Bitch."

We're directed to our very own melamine table, and whilst a waitress hurriedly clears away empty dishes I observe my dining partners. Sandra's tarted right up tonight, she's been a bit over-zealous with the make-up and bats her lengthy false lashes in all directions. Her cleavage pours over a taut, low-cut top like pale blancmange. Marlon is a walking billboard, designer names emblazoned from head to toe: a Voi tee, Diesel jeans and Timberland boots. He sports a much slighter frame than the buff, muscled picture Sandra had painted, and atop it all is a hairless dome, fluorescent reflections catching the dimples of his glistening scalp.

As we look over the drinks menu, Sandra caresses his arm. I stop counting at twenty downward strokes. Everything about this guy seems over-thought. His teak-tone surely came from a tanning salon, and the sapphire blue sparkle of his eyes can only be contact lenses. The corner of his lips curls upwards, giving him a permanent grimace.

It's too early to judge this book by its cover, but he'd already got my back up over that first handshake. Don't people shake hands these days?

Sandra alone chatters through our deep-fried starters. In a vague attempt to cancel out the saturated fats I have flanked mine with some wilting salad. With my first bite into a piece of battered chicken my mouth swims with the taste of old cooking oil and luminous red sweet and sour dipping sauce. Every other item tastes of little more than the grease that killed it.

"Marlon was telling me about all the gays he works with in the hospital!" She pokes his arm, "You should set up our singleton with one!"

"Oh, there's loads of poof –"

From the sharp *THWACK* that comes up from under our table, I feel the kick Sandra gives him.

She whispers loud enough for me to hear, "Only the gays are allowed to use that word Marlon!" A bellowing but embarrassed laugh bursts from her bosom, just as a waiter walking past, laden with a tray of dishes piled high, wobbles, the plates rattle, and the tray topples. I turn away as they smash, and see chunks of white whiz by my feet.

We've yet to delve into the main course, and already I want to leave.

"Ooh, that little disaster reminds me, I've needed a wee since before we got here!" The clip of Sandra's high-heels trails off towards the toilets, leaving Marlon and myself sitting in silence whilst the waiter sweeps the shrapnel up from around us.

"You two met at the hospital?" I say, taking a shot at conversation.

Staring down at his plate and twirling noodles, he grunts. He puts down his fork, picks up his phone and taps away at the screen.

Before her backside hits the chair again Sandra blurts, "We've been talking about moving in together." She jiggles her arm around his shoulder, and pushes her boobs against his bicep.

"But you've only known each other for a few –"

"You wouldn't understand." She swats the air in front of my face. "It just feels right, doesn't it, honey?" She picks up her fork and prods him with it, "I think it would be lovely! Wouldn't it?"

Marlon's face scrunches up. Sandra turns to him, baring puppy eyes along with a cheek-splitting grin, and quickly, his expression drops out, flat.

She always does this. She finds the odd half-decent man, and they're picking out new curtains and matching duvet sets before they've been given the chance to find her G-spot.

"Marlon's staying at mine tonight, aren't ya babes?" She pinches his cheek and he pulls away. "We'll all get a taxi back together."

I wish I had something else to do, someone to meet, somewhere to go. Some paint to watch dry.

Sandra lays her head upon Marlon's shoulder. It reminds me of that photo Aunt Patricia gave me last month, the one I'd stashed away at the back of a drawer.

All the way back I stare out the cab window, scanning the couples drinking, smoking, snogging, groping outside bars and pubs on the Saturday night streets, turned away from the sights and snorts of Sandra molesting her man.

Having slid out of the taxi, Sandra sways on her high heels, grabbing Marlon's arse and giggling like a horny teenager.

"I'll be offski. Was nice to meet you." I decide against formalities or handshakes and start up the road.

"Hold on, you!" Sandra slurs, "Does my lover boy get the thumbs up?"

I grit my teeth. "I reckon he's in for more than just the thumbs up tonight."

Sandra's laugh echoes across the street. "I'll text you tomorrow my lovely gay!"

I step up the pace. And find myself contemplating just how anyone could fuck on a full stomach.

And for one last time tonight, I'm left trying to erase *that* image from my mind.

No. 2 Pencil

by Michelle Elvy

"Got a pencil?" Rick leans across the aisle between the rows of desks toward his friend and holds out his hand.

Stevie reaches for his backpack under his desk. He knows he has an extra pencil – he's got several sharpened No. 2 pencils in his bag, plus a sandwich and an orange. He's pissed about having to come to school on a Sunday to take a test but the test was cancelled yesterday when the fire alarm repeatedly blew and finally the teachers sent everyone home for the day.

And now this – having the misfortune of sitting next to Rick.

He takes longer to pull the extra pencils out than he needs. It's not that he doesn't want to loan Rick the pencil. Or is it? Maybe it's that he doesn't want to loan Rick anything. He's pretty sure he won't get it back. And Rick's been walking around like a douche all semester. He doesn't even act like anything's happened.

As Stevie reaches into his backpack he weighs what he dislikes about Rick, starting with the fact that he knows it was Rick – *Rickie* back then – who stole his Star Wars lunchbox in the seventh grade. It was not from the new series either; it was vintage, from the original *ancient* series from his parents' wonder years. Rick walked around for days talking about how he'd been given a collector's item lunchbox by his Aunt Barbara, but Stevie knew from Manny – his best friend and Rick's cousin – that Aunt Barbara was rarely in the gift-giving mood. Besides, a small dent on the bottom of the lunchbox, right near Luke's shoulder, could only have happened from a drop off the lunch table, which Stevie put there, not Rick. But Rick had been clever enough to keep his new lunchbox at a distance, and eventually Stevie let it go, probably when Rick found something new to brag about.

But there's more. All through Junior High Rick asked Stevie for help with homework. As soon as Stevie would arrive at school, Rick would casually saunter up with a, "Dude, do you have the answers to last night's math?" Or "Let me glance at your history notes, dude." Like it was Stevie's job to help Rick make up for his deficient brain cells. This combined with his bleached blond hair and faux-swimmer's gait was too much. Stevie was an OK swimmer but Rick's blond head sat atop broad swimmer's shoulders and every summer at the community pool he'd strut around with his hair flowing, just because he was on the Junior Lifeguard Squad. Who bleached his hair at age thirteen? Rick – that's who. And he got everyone to notice him, doing a dive off the high dive, or flirting with Marie Wallace. He even got his left hand under her bra at one football game in seventh grade – making him all the more unbearable.

"Dude ..." It's Rick, still leaning across the aisle. "Sucks being here, man. I hate these fuckin' tests. But better'n church, huh?"

Stevie fumbles a little more in his backpack, wants to say *Dude, shut the fuck up* but just ignores Rick and his stupid sense of cool. His mind drifts back to the weekend before the accident, early in January, when Rick told him he was "halfway there" with Ellie Smithers. The way Rick talked about Ellie Smithers made Stevie's blood boil. What the fuck was "halfway" anyway? He wanted to know, and he didn't want to know. He didn't understand why he felt so protective of Ellie. Maybe because she was Lucky's girlfriend. But it was more likely a feeling that nothing good could come of her being anywhere near Rick Sawyer. He sensed a path of self-destruction, and he could only watch from afar. He wasn't close enough to say anything. Sure, they'd talked a few times because she came along pretty often. She'd even asked him once about how to break into a car. He liked that she was interested in his skills. He let himself imagine it meant more than it did.

Then there was the day of the accident, that cold January morning, him being boxed into the back seat next to Ellie and Rick (the memory of it makes his head spin all over again), while Lucky sat up front with Manny, stoned and oblivious. He knew he should be angry at Ellie but he wasn't; he was angry at Rick. He might even hate him. He thinks he does now, anyway, since Rick's been a dick since the accident. He didn't even show up at the funeral. And now it's been months and Rick just struts around with his swimmer shoulders, like the most important thing about this semester is that it's the last one ever for them. Not that the most important thing – the thing Stevie'll never forget about this year – is that Lucky never saw it through.

"He's dead, man, he's fucking dead!" Stevie shouts. But he only shouts it in his own mind. He also pummels Rick's face in his mind – may as well, while he's there. In reality, he's still reaching in his bag and drifting back to January 13. He recalls Lucky's last funny grin, from his passenger seat back to where Stevie sat. He'll never forget that grin. Unlucky Lucky. And then the curve, the flip, the feeling of being airborne, the dream, the floating, the flames, the smell, the turbulent sky and inevitable cornfield where his body touched down. Now he sees his Great-grandpa Gus again, like in the dream, only this time he sees Lucky too, and he can't shake that grin. He'll see it for the rest of his life. Fuckin' Lucky.

A weak sob catches in his chest. He needs air.

"The test will begin in one minute," says a voice from the front of the classroom.

Stevie's fingers wrap around several pencils in his bag. He pulls out a yellow No. 4 from art class, hands it over.

"Here you go, Rickie."

"Thanks, dude."

Country Stars

by Len Kuntz

I wake up in a wheat field, shivering, with something crawling across my face. My first instinct is to flick it away, but I steady myself, as a spider steps over the bridge of my nose.

"You're awake," Heather says. Heather. I picked her up at a cowboy bar back in Fargo and it was her idea to come here because she said the stars from this site were so big they looked like freight cars.

Before the spider can scram, Heather crushes it between her fingers and says, "Your nose is ice cold."

Heather is the first redhead I've ever kissed, ever touched for that matter. Her skin is so freckled it's as if she's been splashed with cinnamon. But she's a bit husky and so some of those freckles look about as big as buttons.

"You hungry?" she asks.

"Not really."

"I'm starving," Heather says, dipping under the sleeping bag and rooting around for my penis.

Afterward, we drive to her place, even though I have a bad feeling about it.

On the way, Heather nuzzles my neck and rubs my thigh and keeps going for my groin, which is more tender than when I was a kid and took a line drive to the crotch. She's leaning on me, making it difficult to drive. "A little room here," I say, but Heather just gets even closer, licking my right nostril.

She lives in a trailer park where the world's skinniest cats slink around heaps of trash, rusted oil drums, abandoned refrigerators and water coolers. Hers is a faded blue thing, shaped like a loaf of bread, near the rear.

I kiss her at the door, feeling sheepish, not knowing how to say goodbye in a way that won't make me seem sleazy.

Heather grabs my wrist so sudden it startles me, and then she's tugging me inside where an enormous woman sits around a table smoking, wearing a corduroy robe that looks to have been gnawed on by a legion of rats.

The woman doesn't bother getting up when I'm introduced, probably because the effort would require a crane.

Heather calls her "Momma." She tells Momma that I'm her boyfriend. "We watched stars all night," Heather says. "Well, not all night," Heather grins, winking.

"Good … for … you … girl," Momma says, the words coming out slow, as if from a stroke victim.

When I say, "We just met," Momma says, "Yeah … shit," and winks at me through a dragon of smoke.

"Come on," Heather says, yanking on my arm again. "My room's in the back."

Her room is only fifteen feet away because this is a very small trailer. I can smell what Momma had for dinner (liver and onions) and when she last used the toilet (very recently). Everything mixes with the pungent odor of cat piss, Budweiser and wet dog.

Heather locks the door behind me, pushing me on her bed so that a cloud of dust fills the air. Her sweater comes off in a jiff before she goes for the zipper on my pants.

71

"Hey," I say, "what are you doing?"

"If you thought you saw God last night, this morning the Holy Ghost is showing up."

"I can't."

"You don't have to do anything. Just lay back and enjoy the rodeo."

"Really," I say, "I can't."

Heather keeps struggling for a grip.

"I mean it."

Then she bites me on the arm.

"What the hell?"

"Let's do it rough."

When I jump off the bed she lunges. I try to shrug her off but she nips at my neck and claws my chin with jagged nails. I hear Momma let out a trombone fart.

"Heather wait, I'm married."

"So am I," she says.

She won't get off me.

"I have herpes," I lie.

"So do I!" she says.

I've never hit a girl in my life, but I don't see how I'm going to get her off me.

"Okay," I say. "Okay, but can I use the bathroom first? I have to pee so bad, I'll never get an erection."

"You can give me a golden shower if you want."

"You're kidding."

"Just don't get any in my eyes."

"I think I'll take a pass on that."

"Spoilsport."

She shows me to the bathroom. It's coat closet-small and reeks of feces. There's a window, but it's tiny and closed and I'd never be able to fit through it, even as skinny as I am.

Heather's shadow is under the door. "Hurry up," she says. "Now I have to go, too."

"I might be a while. I've got to do the other."

"Take a dump?"

I've always hated when people say that, and now it makes me feel filthy. "Yes."

"It doesn't bother me. When nature calls, what're you gonna do?"

"Well, I'm sort of shy about that kind of thing."

"You're shy," Heather chuckles. "Yeah, right."

"A little privacy. Please? Constipated sex is no good."

She thinks this over. "Well, okay, but squeeze that brick out fast as you can. I'll go pee outside."

"Thanks. I'll be done in less than five minutes."

"Better be," she says.

I wait thirty seconds, then fly out of the bathroom, but big Momma has somehow managed to get out of the chair and she's blocking my way, intentionally or otherwise I can't tell, so my only option is to tuck my head and ram her belly. It's like diving into a vat of hamburger. I do it again, using my shoulders, but she only grunts. Finally I grab one of her massive legs and when she falls backward the whole trailer rocks.

Heather comes in buttoning her pants. "What the hell happened?"

"She fell," I say. "I think she might be having a stroke."

"Oh god! Momma!"

When Heather bends down to check on the huge woman, I jump over Momma and sprint out the front door.

"Where are you going?" Heather calls.

Two black Rottweilers come ripping down the road toward me. I make it inside the car and start the motor before they leap against my window. I back out, tires spitting dirt and pebbles. I switch gears and gun the accelerator. One dog flies off the hood, the other squeals. In the rearview Heather is running after me, shouting and waving her arm, holding what looks to be a butcher's knife.

73

Tuesday, 15th April 2014

Fourth Inning

by Michael Webb

It isn't baseball weather. Grey and forbidding, with a misting rain falling out of low, angry clouds, it's soup and blanket weather for most, but just another early season day in another city for us. Nobody wants to play – not the sparse group of diehard fans huddled under cover; not the umpires, huddled inside until the last possible moment; not the grounds crew warming their hands over the hot dog steam; and certainly not the players, conscious of the fragile bodies they are compensated so well for using. But the remorseless logic of the schedule, which doesn't bring us back here until August, forces us to try and play.

I come out to test the air, immediately concluding that I need another layer. I go back down the tunnel, the concrete wet, the black plastic across the floor clotted with mud and grass and spilled Gatorade already. The visitors' clubhouse is in muted grays and blues, with black partitions for dressing. I make my way through the nearly empty room, the rest of my mates already plodding around the wet field, or stomping and shivering in the dugout behind me. The sweatshirt I want is gone from the hook where I left it, filched by a comrade who didn't want to look for his own. I glance around, but none are available, so I look into the trainer's room.

I recognize immediately the bare back and shaggy mane of Tex Holman, our new flame-throwing bullpen savior, his muscles impressively laid out around a Texas Longhorns tattoo at the small of his back. He makes a hissing sound, straightening up with what looks like a syringe in his enormous right hand. The plunger is down, and he withdraws the needle from his quadriceps with practiced speed, rubbing the spot briskly with his other palm.

He senses me and twists halfway around.

"Twainie!" he says in his friendliest tone. "Just a little B12, man." In the faux casual world of baseball, even nicknames have nicknames, so my nom de guerre, Mark Twain, because of my habit of reading on planes and buses, becomes "Twainie".

"B12?" I say, nodding. "Sure. Just getting a sweatshirt." I take one from the pile on a side table, checking the size on the tag then slipping it on over my head. "Cold as hell, man," I say conversationally.

"Yeah?" the huge reliever says, standing to his full height, broad and thick like a pro wrestler. He pulls up his uniform pants, staring back at me. "Thanks for the update."

"Alright," I say, backing out the door. "See you out there."

"You bet, MT." His exalted role on the team means he doesn't have to join the bullpen until the game is half over. Less well-paid and more fungible commodities like me have to spend the whole game out there. I walk back down the corridor, and then out onto the field, trudging out onto the slick surface.

It could have been B12, but who self-administers something unless you want to keep it quiet? Simple self-interest tells me to keep my own counsel – a winning team raises all boats, which means we all get wealthier. And clubhouse omerta says the same – in the insular world of baseball, a reputation as a snitch gets you frozen out as quickly as a fading fastball would.

I am envious of his hulking physique, the simple equalizer of being able to put the ball up there into the triple digits in a tight spot. I'd love to have his endorsements, his fashion model girlfriends, his talk show popularity. I know, or I think I know, that he got there by skirting the rules. I am confident he is going to take his money and, after his elbow comes apart like a truck tire on the highway, live out his life as the former star felled by injury. On the rare occasion that someone asks about steroids, I use the old chestnut that I want to be able to look my children in the face and tell them I tried my hardest without bending the rules. I think about my children, their open faces and their belief that everyone plays fair, and I think about how Holman makes more in a month than I make in half a year, and I keep trudging towards the bullpen in the soaking mist.

A Dose of the Leather

by James Claffey

The windows are covered with frost and the Bird sees his breath in the air as he exhales. Melodie went back home to France last week when she found out her brother had a stroke and was in a coma. He touches the place setting where she had sat the evening before she took off for the ferry – a lace doily of his mother's – and kissed him farewell in the hall. Oh, well, he thinks, stripping the linens from the table and getting the sandpaper out of his toolbox. It's about time the table was sanded and stained again, he thinks, and sets about turning the dark stained wood to pale. He doesn't notice the frost melting and the steam rising from the road outside. Instead he says her name on each push of sandpaper – Melodie, in. Melodie, out. Melodie, in. Melodie, out.

With the table stripped of varnish he settles down in the parlor and sups a glass of stout. The floor is patterned with sawdust and he trails the toe of his shoe in the dust, spelling out her name. After several minutes he stops, pushes back his chair, and drags a foot through the crude letters. "To hell with her!" he shouts, and takes his hat and coat from the rack, all set for the snug of the nearest bar. Nothing like a quiet spot on a chilly Wednesday in Lent. This is the first year he's not given up the drop for the season, what with the Mammy and Daddy dead and buried there's no one to hold him to the pledge.

Trade is slow in McEgan's, the religious weight of the season keeping all but the reckless and the few Protestants in town from their sup. The Bird casts his mind on the strange dreams of his mother he's been plagued with since her death. Some of them so vivid he could almost touch the apparition, the dreams sent him to the doctor, who looked with interest in the Bird's ears and nose, as if searching for traces of his mother's ghost. At the end of the examination, the doctor rubbed his hands together at speed, and declared the Bird to be "as fit as a fiddle," and to "pay no attention to visitors in the night time, unless they're attractive young ladies scantily clad." He sips from the pint and pulls at the long stiff hairs coming out of his ears. Nervous tics are the Bird's refuge and he finds the incessant stroking of these hairs to be calming.

Enough taken as far as drink goes, the Bird steps out into the cold air and strolls down to Mahony's turf accountants to place a few bob on a tip he got from the priest after Sunday Mass. "Goldfinch, two quid each way," he tells the spotty young lad behind the glass as he pushes his few notes across the counter. Receipt in hand, he nestles into a corner and waits for the race to begin. Three or four other men, all clad in raincoats and Wellingtons, hold copies of the *Racing Post* and wear intense looks. The commentator on the TV calls the race, and out of the gate the Goldfinch meanders along behind the rest of the horses. "Get up, you bitch," the Bird hisses. The other men appear not to have a stake in the same horse as the Bird. They slap folded newspapers against palms and thighs, egging their charges forward.

As the horses near the last turn, Goldfinch is twenty lengths behind the pack and the Bird tears his ticket stub into flitters. So much for the doctor's "tip." The man wouldn't know a decent horse if it bit him on the arse. The

Bird confettis the ticket into the trash and heads off into the grey of the afternoon.

Over the steeple of the church the sun does its best to lighten the afternoon, like an old friend attempting to give solace to the bereaved. The clouds thicken once more and a rain shower sheds its weight on the village. The Bird wishes he could transport himself all the way to Melodie's side and enjoy the confusion of listening to a language he cannot comprehend. She told him she might not be back for months, at least until her brother's diagnosis is clear. Unlike the Bird's, Melodie's parents are alive and well, in a small rural town near Le Havre.

He perches on a bench along the church wall, the stones mossy and damp, a few starlings dotting the low branches of the old oaks. All around him the smell and feel of spring, a few daffodils poking their butter yellow blooms into the air, the scent of softer earth now the thaw is here, and all he can think about is how much he misses her. Odd, he thinks, how he'd never had those feelings for another woman before. When his mammy had been alive the Bird rarely found himself in the company of unmarried women, having to always be around the house in case either of his parents needed an errand run. As a lad he'd gone to a few hops in the local GAA club on a Saturday night, but the loud music and the smoky room didn't suit him at all. From the bench he watches the few cars and bicycles pass by on the street, raising a hand in greeting every so often. Not a bad life, he thinks. Not bad.

The local schoolteacher rides past on her bicycle and the Bird remembers his own classroom days, the batterings from the teachers, the sting of the leather strap the headmaster used on the boys. Nothing like a dose of the leather to make you toe the line, he thinks. As he sits on the bench he takes in the changes in the town, the new video rental shop, the fancy German grocery, the boarded-up cobbler's shop where he'd go as a lad and inhale the glue and leather smell with relish. There was a time when a stranger like Melodie would have been as rare as a hen's tooth, but now, with the Eurozone and all that, well, there are foreigners in every crevice of the country. Fair play, the Bird thinks, picturing the lovely smile he wishes he could reach out and touch.

The Bird unmoors from the bench and wanders down to the river where mallards float unmoved by the cold. His daddy loved the ducks, always bringing the Bird along with him on Sunday afternoons, a bag of breadcrumbs in his pocket, relishing the way the ducks would line up at their feet for a sprinkling of food. In the water, the ripples from a diving bird spread outward in circles, and in the broken mirror of the past the Bird sees his father holding his hand, the bread dropping like snow into the throng of waiting ducks.

The Rules We Shall Die By

by Gwendolyn Joyce Mintz

"Vince says he's not coming," Aaron tells the group when he returns to the table. He was outside making a call. He plops down, slips his cell phone in his shirt pocket and alternates a glare between Diane and Phil. "What did you two do?"

Diane frowns at him. "We didn't *do* anything. We simply stated an opinion: you shouldn't be selfish when you kill yourself. You can think about others." She leans back in the booth, crosses her arms in front of her. "He's not nice, anyway; he said I knew way too much about celebrity deaths."

"You do," Mora says from across the table.

"You know they fascinate me," Diane replies without turning to her friend.

"Why is that?" Phil asks. "I was gonna ask the last time but then Vince said you should spend more time on your own death and things just went downhill."

Mora answers for Diane. "Things that she doesn't understand make her crazy so she obsesses over them in an effort to understand."

"We think celebrities have everything, but they must not if some would rather die than enjoy said things," Diane adds.

Phil nods.

Aaron waits a moment. "Okay, but back to Vince."

"If he wanted to die, he would have made it."

Aaron is about to reply but Diane continues, "You said some meetings ago that if you want to die, this is the place to be. So he's obviously not as committed or he'd be here."

"Yep," Mora says.

Aaron shoots her a look that suggests she needn't chime in.

She smiles at him. "What?" she says.

"I thought we were going to talk about dying and getting it done," Diane says.

With a sigh, Aaron nods in agreement. "I know, I know. The rate I'm going, I might be alive come January."

Mora covers his hand with hers.

Aaron takes a breath. Her touch. He inches his hand from under hers. "So what do we do now?"

"Well, I'd like for us to talk about the reasons why we want to die," Phil offers.

Diane nods. "We need to tell our stories."

"I'm still undecided," Mora tells them, "but I do want to bear witness to your journeys."

Diane smiles. "That's beautiful," she says before turning to Aaron. "Did you think about some rules, like I suggested, you being the de facto president of the club?"

"I did some thinking, yes. Like, are we going to say goodbye?"

"I think we should," Diane answers. "A group text isn't too much to ask. I can do that while the pills take effect." She giggles.

Mora shakes her head, rolls her eyes.

"Okay, okay." Aaron signals the server, asks for something to write on and with.

She returns with several sheets of copier paper and a pen.

Aaron scribbles on the page. "What about funerals? Do we attend?"

After considering it, Mora says, "It might be awkward; it's not like you could say, 'I'm glad they finally did it.'"

There's murmuring among them as the group agrees.

Aaron continues to write.

After some time, he sets the pen down and pushes a page to the center of the table. "It's a start," he says.

Diane lifts the page and reads. She nods. She asks Aaron for the pen, then she signs her name. She passes the paper and pen to Phil. He reads, signs and hands the sheet to Mora.

She signs.

"We can amend or add as time goes on. If more people join," Aaron says. "But for now these are the rules we shall die by." He takes the page from Mora and rereads what he's written.

We, the undersigned, agree to the following:

1. *When we decide that our time to die has come, we will contact the other members of "The Suicide Club" and let them know. We agree that we will simply say 'goodbye.'*
2. *We will not attend any memorial service or funeral related to any member. We will celebrate any and all former members of "The Suicide Club" at the next monthly meeting.*
3. *We will not discuss with any one, other than the members of the club, any deaths that have occurred.*
4. *We will support each member in his or her efforts to end his or her life. Rather than report any member to any organization which would deter said member from his or her wishes, each of us agrees to leave the club instead.*
5. *We will not judge what has brought members here.*
6. *We will hold what happens at any meeting as well as what is said in strict confidence.*

"We should wrap up on this note," Aaron tells them. "It feels right." He sets the paper down.

As they stand, Mora asks, "Are you going to conduct another membership drive?"

Aaron laughs. "No, I just think that there may be others like us and it doesn't seem right, somehow, for this club to just die with us."

That Earthy Trace

by Stephen V. Ramey

I sip coffee from a sampling cup. The taste is heavy, slightly sweet, a hint of clay. What better way to kick off Good Friday?

"Sumatra Lintong," the barista says. "Do you like it?" She's a perky redhead with a generous smile. Her nametag says *Sara*. What I like is the way her attention remains on me even as other customers line up. The world has enough multi-taskers.

"Pour me a double," I say.

Sara turns to the machine. I look around. The Confluence is relatively new, and quite ambitious for New Castle, a cavernous community center / coffee shop / art studio in the downtown historic district. It stays busy and attracts a younger crowd, but probably not busy enough or young enough. For years New Castle has been struggling to change its identity. We're the city that time and politics destroyed, the city that does not deserve better.

Opposite the coffee area is a low stage. I keep meaning to come down here to see a local band. So many things I keep meaning to do. Right now, I'm supposed to be at a doctor's appointment, a urologist to be precise. He gave me prostate cancer materials to research last time, and I'm supposed to decide on a treatment regimen today. I'm not good at decisions. So here I sit in The Confluence a half-hour after my appointment, cell phone turned off in my pocket. I have no idea what I'll tell Anne, but I'm a writer, I'll think of something. Maybe I'll say I'm cured. *It's a damned miracle.* Like Jesus rising on the third day.

Sara sets a cup before me. I reach for my wallet, only to see Anne walking through the front door. Panic deep-freezes my bowels. *My God, she heard me thinking!* Head down, I start toward the back of the building.

"Hey," Sara says.

Shit. I grab a bill from the wallet.

"Don't you want your change?" She stretches a twenty between her hands. *Great.* At the door, Anne frowns. She's seen me, or thinks she has.

"Keep it." I drag the cell phone from my pocket and pretend to answer as I duck behind a section of staggered wall. I should have remembered Anne had an Earth Day meeting this morning. It was on the calendar: *Confluence 9:30 – Earth Day.* She's been working with a planning committee for six months now. How stupid of me to come here. What was I thinking?

Fortunately the back door isn't locked. I push through and risk a glance back as it hisses closed. Anne is coming. She does not look happy.

I feel like a bug caught on the counter when the light snaps on. Riverplex Park is a y-shaped expanse of concrete bound by wrought iron fence on one side and a busy road on the other. There's no place to hide. Then, I see yellow tape, an opening in the fence. *Yes!* The Riverwalk is under construction, crews cleaning up the bank for the new boardwalk.

I run, duck under the tape, and scramble down a path toward the river. Stones sprinkle. Minnows scatter. I pass through the underbelly shadow of a concrete bridge. Cars rumble above. On the opposite side people in orange vests pull weeds. A stocky man gives me a look, but doesn't try to stop me. Maybe it's no skin off his nose if I get poison ivy or drown. Or maybe, and I like this better, it's because I seem unstoppable.

The bank narrows until I'm mere inches from the river. A gurgle fills the basin. My stomach relaxes. I feel safe in this wrinkle hidden from the surface, water carrying the moment away as soon as it arrives. My witch friend, Rose, once said that I should live in the moment if I want to find peace. That's not easy for me. It's never the word at my fingertips that matters, but the word coming next, or the words already published below my byline.

My prostate gland – what I imagine it to be – shoots a sting through my body. I slow. Pain settles to a steady itch. I want to probe up there and scratch it, feel nodes flake away like dust. I want to be well. I want it to be over.

A patch of suds floats by, fertilizer or detergent or something else that does not belong. I think of Anne making my appointments, cooking my meals, cuddling me as I lay in bed worrying before sleep. She deserves so much better.

"Who the fuck are you?" A man in fatigues steps onto the path. Panic jolts me. I take a step back, but why? The city is a half-block away – I hear the traffic – and he's not exactly threatening. His frame is like scaffolding, his gaunt face scabbed. I'm thinking meth-head, but his eyes are very clear, very focused.

"You undercover?" he says. "Nah, you're no cop. Come here to party? What'd you bring?"

My hand goes to my back pocket. "I have a little cash, if that's what you want." I'm glad I gave the twenty to Sara.

The man shrugs. "Name's Scanner, what's yours?"

"I … Stephen." Explanations ebb into my thoughts. *I'm taking a stroll, looking for my dog, I'm lost.* I remember the rich aroma of coffee, Sara's smile. Honest things. "I'm a writer."

"You writing an article for *The News*?" Scanner says.

"I'm not exactly sure."

"Come on," he says. "I'll show you around Tent City. You like beer? We got a case of *Colt 45* this morning. We share stuff like that." He nods at the shirt pocket where I keep my idea notepad. "You want to write that down?"

"Later." I feel a shiver coming on and stamp my feet.

Scanner leads me into a cluster of budding maples and stunted black oaks a few yards from the river. A hand-made *No Trespasing* sign is stapled to one. I wonder if maybe I *should* write an article. I could use the distraction. No, that's what I always do. I need to stay focused on the novel.

We enter a clearing that smells of fish. Plywood lean-tos draped in plastic tarp form a ragged line. A bald man lies on his back under one.

"Stay away from him," Scanner says. "Don't know his name yet, just came down from Pittsburgh, eye all messed up. I think he's got the PTSDs."

A man sits in the next tent, shoulders curled forward.

"That's Jake," Scanner says. "He'll sober up in the afternoon. You should talk to him then, used to be a social worker, knows where the skeletons are and like that." He angles toward the neatest of the tents. "I'll take you to Tamara. She's the one you want to talk to first."

I don't actually want to talk to anyone, but a woman pushes out from the tarp right on cue. She's huge, taller than me, twice as broad. Her stringy hair is brown-red, the skin of her broad face pocked like a cratered moon. Her fringed leather jacket reminds me of the seventies.

"This is Stephen," Scanner says. "He's a writer, Tamara."

Tamara looks me over. "You're here to write?"

"Sure he is," Scanner says. "The glasses, the notebook in his pocket?" He nods to me. "Tell her you're a writer, Stephen."

I open my mouth – I *am* a writer – but Tamara's steady gaze stops me. "I don't know why I came."

She nods. "I sense your pain. You're alone, you want to join us. Was your home foreclosed?"

"I'm dying," I mumble. "Stage 4 cancer." Sadness numbs my senses. I want to curl onto the ground and cry, but I can't do that, not here in front of strangers.

"Hell, man, *everyone's* dying," Scanner says. "Some just don't notice it so much."

"My wife," I choke. I imagine Anne's blazing eyes, the fire of her determination. She won't let me die.

Tamara takes a tarnished flask from her pocket and presses it into my palm. "Drink this, Stephen. It will help."

I expect whiskey, but it's water, cold and sharp without a hint of chlorine.

"The river called you," Tamara says. "The blood and tears of Mother Earth, who holds us up when we would fall." She takes the flask back. "You should go now, Stephen. Come back when you're ready."

Flipping Out

by Gay Degani

Charmaine snorts at the mushroom smell of wet grout and curses her husband. White tile! Not even subway! Didn't she force him to watch hours of prerecorded HGTV just to avoid this kind of mistake? Marble equals updated. Tile, not so much. And still, he has the guy install it behind her back, while she's at his sister's fucking baby shower!

She pivots away, can't stand the sight of it, and bangs her toe. A tool, of course, one of Sam's. Left on the floor, not put away. She stoops and snatches the hammer, its wood handle smooth with age. Rust speckles the worn head, the curved claw. She tosses it hard onto the counter and it lands with a crack. She looks. Grins. Broken square of tile. Good. Serves him right.

But more than this is broken. Everything's broken. She growls. How she'd loved this house when they were scraping together the down payment, when all she saw was potential. Now she's overwhelmed with mold snaking through the basement, termites camped in the attic, the plumber who fell through the dining room ceiling, the gush of water that followed him down. Funny at the time, but the aftermath, the damage, the money, the delay ...

She stalks into the bedroom where an air mattress fills one corner and throws herself onto the puddle of sheets. She wishes it wasn't Saturday, wishes Sam wasn't outside chopping up what's left of the sycamore that fell last January. She wants to wallow and he hates to see her wallow. But wouldn't that punish him for his thoughtlessness? How he tricked her while she was off witnessing his sister's glowing happiness? Is wallowing enough?

A thought makes her shiver. She knows she can't resist this urge. Doesn't want to.

In the bathroom, she lifts the hammer above her shoulder, catches sight of her face in the mirror. Her cheeks are flushed, her eyes glassy, a thick strand of brown hair bisects her face. She bends down, runs a hand roughly from the back of her scalp to the top, then tosses her head. Yes. This is who she is, the powerful woman in the glass, wielding her weapon, and smirking, she smacks the hammer down, shatters each shiny new tile one by one. Chips of ceramic fly off, skid across the counter onto the floor as she moves faster and faster.

"Charmaine!"

She spins around and there's Sam, blocking the doorway, face spotted with dirt, hair sweat-damp, body odor rolling off him. She has a right to show anger. A right to put him in his place. She says, "See what happens when you don't listen to me? When I say marble, I mean *marble*." She finishes with a flourish by holding up the hammer and moving toward him, everything a blur until she's close enough to feel his heat, close enough to experience a tremor of fear – has she gone too far this time? But he steps out of her way, back into the bedroom. Her heart pounds and her foot falters, but she keeps walking.

Out the front door she goes, almost running, but reining it in, exhilarated with triumph, the sun vying with rain, the devil beating his wife, as her mother used to say. She trembles, pitches the hammer onto the lawn, watches it thud. Then, clutching her arms around herself, she strides past Sam's tidy stack of cut wood and onto the sidewalk.

She doesn't know where she's going, but she *can't* go back inside. Not yet. She looks up and down the Old Road and spies a neighbor, that old man who's always walking his dog, coming up from the creek. She glances around, and hurries toward the only place out of the open, up the short walkway to the green gate of the Trencher house that separates her own fixer-upper from the bungalows. She fumbles with the latch and ducks inside.

Like most of the yards on the Old Road, this one is weedy, but the owners have gone overseas, England, she thinks, or Wales, and won't be back, according to Sam who, unlike her, enjoys the occasional chat with neighbors. She surveys the two-story Mediterranean, noting the tile roof in need of repair, the faded blue shutters, an arched entryway built like the entrance into a Spanish fort. The house is appealing in spite of the dead bushes, crumbling paint, and broken window on the second floor. This is a place just waiting to be flipped, much more potential than her own little cottage with its tacky kitchen and wormy wood.

Sam. Is he following her? She can't tell and she's afraid to look. She will explode if she has to endure, even for a second, the sympathy in his eyes. She wishes he'd just shake her, throw her on the floor, kick her in the belly, and leave. Damn him. Damn him.

She wipes her nose. The front door has one of those key boxes on it. There's no "For Sale" sign planted in the yard, and Charmaine figures the realtor is lazy or new on the job and maybe, just maybe, the box is open, the key inside. She steals up the walkway, and with a glance at the empty street, she checks the box. The contraption is shut and locked, doesn't yield to her tug. She fingers each dial as if she's cracking a safe code to no avail. She stamps her foot, tastes blood in her mouth.

Up the driveway and into the unkempt back yard she goes, surveying the lower windows, grinning when she sees

French doors leading from a cracked cement patio into the house. A glance yields an assortment of fallen branches the right size for her use. In this moment, she considers the January windstorm a blessing, sent to her by a forgiving god who loves her and only her. Making up perhaps for what he's taken away. She weighs one limb and then another and selects the one that most resembles a baseball bat.

Reflected in the double doors her image is divided into twelve square panes, and like in the bathroom mirror, she rejoices in the powerful figure she sees. "Towanda on a rampage" passes through her head from some forgotten movie, and with the end of the branch she breaks the glass, one pane splintering at a time. She reaches in and tries the door, but it's bolted. The branch now a battering ram, she smashes out each slat of wood – bam – bam – bam! – until the hole is large enough for her to stoop inside.

In the late afternoon light, she can barely make out the table and chairs in the center of the room. She searches for a light switch, finds one, flicks it back and forth. No lights come on. But down the hall, rosy sunlight draws her into the huge living room. Hardwood floors, a plastered fireplace at the far end, gorgeous tile which smudges her fingertips with soot. She sees herself emptying the house of its hideous furniture, pulling down the heavy velvet curtains, restoring the vaulted ceiling, filling the rooms with antiques.

Her hand runs over worn mahogany as she climbs the winding staircase, reminding her of the hammer handle, polished by years of contact with skin. If they owned this house, she'd take up the threadbare carpeting, put down a Persian runner, add those brass bars that fit neatly at the back of each step. She could work wonders here.

At the top, on the large landing, the setting sun stains the stucco walls red, and Charmaine hesitates, a ghost hand on her shoulder, holding her back. In the distance, Sam calls her name as if she were a missing pet, and grimacing, she steps into the nearest bedroom.

She knows what kind of room this is, a mobile outlined against the darkening afternoon, a zoo of stuffed animals lining a window seat, and the crib that she could touch if she only would. She can't move except for breath, her heart shattering like white ceramic tile and twelve square panes of glass.

Sunday, 20th April 2014

And no one told me!

by Sally-Anne Macomber

To: Milton Flaxmill, Red Cow Publishing
From: Trudy Polaris
Date: April 20, 2014 1:18 a.m.
Re: Developments

Hi Milton,

I emailed you the plane ticket and waited for you at Langkampfen Airport but you didn't arrive. I was sitting for a long time on an orange vinyl seat staring at white floor tiles listening to the arrivals in German but that's OK because I've started editing *Nuclear Fission in the Pyrénées* while I wait for you to get here. (I'm not at the airport any longer by the way.) I'm hoping to get the word count down to 80,000 words. It started at about 81,226 – just in case you'd forgotten – but I have my best 'another person with other eyes' hat on and I think I'll have the book in good shape by the time you get here.

So it will be good to know *when* you will get here.

I'm establishing a routine. After the milking is finished, I have a cup of coffee sitting beside the computer and I slowly work my way through each page of the text and I'm cutting words out at a great rate. Then I drink the coffee and put most of the words back in.

But you will be pleased to know I am also learning a lot about local fashion and through a connection in the *dirndl* industry I heard there was an opening as a representative for the local cheese board. So my new job as the Tyrolean Fetta Ambassadress starts next week.

Between the milking and this new cheese job my time editing the book will be limited but rest assured, I am fully committed and intend using my time well by developing new skills as a power-editor. I signed up for the course yesterday.

And now the bad news. I thought we would be here in our Tyrolean hideaway for only a few weeks but my husband revealed we have to stay here for a while longer, for tax reasons. I am desperate to leave: there's only so many Alpine goats I can milk every morning! (And they're goats, they're not cows, they're goats! Large goats! And no one told me!)

So quite without any input from me, I've become a tax hostage!

I am trying not to let this get me down. The thought of a kindred spirit (i.e. you) sitting beside me in my Alpine writer's paradise, sharing writerly jokes (*Why did the chicken cross the road? Because he was reading!*) raises my spirits. But at the moment that's just a thought. And while we are taught *it's the thought that counts*, the reality is you are in Boston and I am here in the Tyrol ... so it will be good and probably even a relief when we finally meet. (And I thought we were only coming here for the February skiing season!)

On another but related point, I think it would be better to change the title to *Nuclear Fission in The Pyrénées*, that's with a 'T' on The Pyrénées, you know what I mean, a capital 't' (I mean 'T') on The Pyrénées.

I have put it in bold here – **The Pyrénées** – just so you know what I mean.

Hoping you get this email and that there's not a black email hole at Red Cow Publishing nor is there more than one Milton Flaxmill at Red Cow Publishing and I am sending this to the wrong Milton Flaxmill.

Well, auf Wiedersehen again, and glad to know we're still on the same page,

Trudy

Snakes in April

by Mandy Nicol

Mum cranes her neck over the back of the car seat to check Peregrine. I can't see him in the rear view mirror but I can hear him panting. Poor dog.

"Can't you go any faster Nadia?" she says for the tenth time.

"Not legally," I say. I'm varying my responses, treating it like one of those games kids play on long drives to pass the time, like counting McDonalds Restaurants or Volkswagen Beetles. On this road they'd have to count gum trees or magpies or cattle grids.

"What are snakes doing out this late in April anyway?" she asks.

"We're not sure it was a snake, Mum."

"Of course it was a snake."

I don't argue. Maybe it was a snake.

"It's all this global warming," she says. "It's turning everything upside down. First we had to put on the heater on Christmas Day and now there are snakes out and about in April. Snakes in April!"

I don't argue. Maybe global warming has messed up their hibernation pattern.

"It's all those mice in the hay shed," she says. "That's what brings them in the first place. If you'd put out poison like I told you to this wouldn't have happened. You know Peregrine's always hunting around in that hay shed."

I don't argue. I don't say if I'd put out poison we'd probably be making the same trip because Peregrine had scoffed it. Though he probably wouldn't have done it on Easter Monday, which would have saved me a heap on the vet bill, and would have stopped the vet from being pissed off at being called to his surgery on a Public Holiday.

We hit town and I slow to sixty. "A lot of dogs survive snake bite," I say.

"And a lot more don't," says Mum. She cranes her neck to check the speedo.

I turn to check Peregrine. He's still panting and drooling but at least he's alive. He'd be dead by now if he'd been bitten by a Brown, the vet had said as much on the telephone.

"Then let's hope Peregrine's one of the lucky ones," I say.

Mum peers at me over her glasses. "Can't you go any faster, Nadia?"

Dr. Stanley Runs Late

by Margaret Bingel

Dr. Stanley looks at his calendar. He is running late for his 1:00pm appointment with Ned Billingsly. He logs out of the app on his iPhone, and while waving a waiter down, he remembers he has 12 minutes to get across 20 blocks of city traffic. Dr. Stanley throws a fifty down and runs out the door. He flags down the nearest taxi, he gives the driver the address for St. Jude's, then settles into the backseat and thinks about his patient.

Dr. Stanley knows all about the ex-coma patient: having been in a two month coma, Mr. Billingsly has been recovering quickly, first by sitting up in bed by himself, then rising to his feet unassisted, even if for a few minutes. For two weeks they have been working on walking, Dr. Stanley standing next to him as he shuffles each slippered step down the therapy ramp. Hopefully, we can work on actually lifting the foot up soon, or else his ankles will never recover properly, Dr. Stanley thinks, as he wrings his hands. Somehow, the driver has hit every red light possible, making his passenger squirm in his seat. Not being on time bothers Dr. Stanley.

Despite Ned's smooth road to recovery, it's his conflicting reports of Ned's attitude that bothers Dr. Stanley the most. Even with x-rays and CT scans, there doesn't appear to be any brain damage, but his mother, Nora, believes that there has to be something wrong with her son. *My boy*, Dr. Stanley remembers, *is not my boy anymore.*

"But that's the way it is with sons, Mrs. Billingsly," Dr. Stanley said that first day he met Nora and her 'troubled boy'. "Once they reach a certain age, they become men."

He smiles, a reassuring smirk he uses for fearful patients and their families. He remembers her eyebrows knotting when he had said, "Mrs." Perhaps she isn't married, he had thought.

"But you don't know my son," Nora had said, her gray eyes flashing. "My son has never been determined in his life. No direction, always complacent. This isn't like him at all!" The wrinkles on her forehead looked like a bow on a birthday present, but her eyes were a dammed river. "He doesn't even smile."

Dr. Stanley sighs as he remembers the sound of Nora's voice. One time he purposely walked in on her reading to her son while he lay in bed, Ned's hands in fists. It was a Saturday, a day he knew she would be visiting, and he showed up early, just to hear her read. When Dr. Stanley leaned in closer to the door, Nora heard the linoleum squeak. He told her that he loved *The Wizard of Oz*, and she smiled. He smiles out the window, thinking of Nora's face.

The taxi pulls up to the curb. Dr. Stanley gives the driver a twenty, and, slamming the car door, rushes into St. Jude's, slowing to a walk once he enters the building. Jumping over every other step, he arrives on the fourth floor, the rehab clinic, and walks into Room 231, where Mr. Billingsly is waiting for him.

Dr. Stanley pulls out his phone and looks at the time. 1:05pm. *Shit*, he swears under his breath. He looks up at Nora's son (disappointing, he doesn't have her eyes) and gives him one of his smirks.

"Sorry, I'm late, Mr. Billingsly. Shall we get started?"

"Let's," answers Ned, with a smile.

It's Bright in Here

by Darryl Price

Close the door. Oh yeah there are no doors, or none that I can see. Maybe you're blocking the doors. Do you think I'm going to try to escape? Listen, if I thought I could escape I would have been gone a long time ago.

You wanted me to write things down, so that's what I'm doing. I'm being a good boy.

Without her my bed is a tomb. Any wind is a slap in the face. My food is poison.

What do you want me to say?

Okay. Here it is. I built a house for her. No not in the so-called real world, so don't try to lay that on me, but it was every bit as real to me. I could see it, I could feel it, I could care about it. But that collapsed in on me, too, because nothing holds up without her being there. Every nut and bolt is a lie. I can't help this. That sky is a lie. For instance. It's nothing but a poster taped to a window. That outside bird is a lie. An unfortunate scar in the butter of sunlight. My own hands on the sheets dead beside me are like discarded shoes looking for a box. Don't you get it? I'm sorry. I should have told you this kind of thinking upsets me.

You wanted me to tell you a story. All stories are lies. But perhaps they contain a bit of truth.

How did I get here?

I don't belong here.

Okay. OK. Let's get down to it. I made a mistake. Someone used to love me.

Someone I miss. I can't stop missing. It's messed me up. I see that now. I just want to go home and sit on a couch and eat some ice cream and sleep or watch TV. All this groveling for answers isn't going to get us anywhere. Because she's gone, just like the record says. And I can't deal with it like I should, or like you want me to.

Is that so wrong?

Okay, ok, let me give it another go. She died. I lived. End of story. No? No? No no no no no no no no. I want to be the one who dies. She has every reason to live. I'm the one you wanted. You got the wrong person. I'm ready to go.

Give me a few minutes alone to think this thing out. I'll try again later. I've got plenty of paper and this hospital pen, if that's what this place is.

Maybe this isn't earth at all.

That would make the most sense.

Did you give me something? Cause I'm starting to feel mighty sleepy. That's a word you don't hear much anymore. Mighty. Like Mighty Mouse. You probably never even heard of him, but he saved the day.

Once.

Patience

by Teresa Burns Gunther

Rachel whips around a too slow car on US101, cuts past a pickup, crosses two lanes and exits the freeway. "Jesus," Gail gasps, clutching the passenger door with one hand, a box to her belly with the other. *Patience* Rachel reminds herself. She's wasting her lunch hour to do her officemate a favor.

Gail's a tax fraud specialist, too; a mousy thing who tries but that morning she overslept, arrived late to the office, a rumpled flurry in a gray business suit, her brown hair oily and flat against her head. Rachel has no patience with slovenliness; she is always well-groomed in a crisp suit and heels.

She zips through the intersection on Army Street two seconds after the yellow light flashes red. Gail gives sounds to her nervous state. Though the day is thick with fog, Rachel has the windows down blowing her hair into havoc, because Gail's mission stinks. She takes her hands off the wheel, pulls her hair into a twist she tucks down her blouse. Gail reaches for the wheel but Rachel blocks her in time.

Patience is Rachel's 2014 resolution for April. So when Gail, who shares her 40-hour-a-week slice of IRS paradise needed help with her mission and begged her for a ride at lunch Rachel said yes, enjoying Gail's wide-eyed surprise. It's good practice and besides, the stink and scritchscratching in their office from the box Gail holds was more than she could take. "It better not mess up my car," Rachel warns again.

Gail clucks her tongue. Rachel got Gail's text: *Cover 4 me?* on her way into the staff meeting. Now Gail's pissed that Rachel told everyone Gail was late because she had cramps and needed tampons. It was the first excuse that came to mind. Everyone acted amused though her boss, the arrogant ironman, actually seemed impressed. He'd denied Rachel a raise the previous fall claiming she lacked people skills. Apparently, covering for slacker employees is what he's after. Patience is clearly part of the people skills calculus, though numbers, she thinks, are so much easier to work with. "What did you want me to say?" she asks Gail.

"A dentist appointment would have sufficed."

Rachel shrugs. "Next time, be specific. I'm not practiced in deception."

"Clearly," Gail says.

Rachel and Gail aren't chummy. They don't *do* lunch and Rachel rarely joins the after work cocktail coven and gossip. She's always been impatient with Gail's ups, downs, and daily dramas. And today's drama is the bird Gail rescued on her way to work. The closest bird sanctuary is in Oakland, and though it's only a ten-minute zip over the Bay Bridge at mid-day it's closed on Thursdays. Rachel tells her "never fear" and heads for her neighbors' house.

"You can give it to the Aussies: Joyce and Larry," she explains. "They have a zoo in their backyard – *rabbits for eating, chooks not for eating*, and lots of *fruits and veg*." She mimics their lazy Australian accent and confused vowels.

Gail looks skeptical. "Didn't your dog kill and eat their rabbit?"

"Stella didn't eat it and it was already dead," Rachel says.

When she finally pulls into her narrow driveway with a screech Gail's eyes are closed, her hand white-knuckled on the door.

"Let's go."

Gail lingers, sizing up Rachel's white house with its blue trim and flowering window boxes, but Rachel shoos her up the neighbors' front stairs to the porch jungled up with morning glories and begonias.

Joyce opens the door and smiles at Gail, her broad face smiling, curious, until she catches sight of Rachel. Her eyes narrow, she crosses her arms over her vast bosom. Joyce hasn't said word one to her since the rabbit incident. Rachel had hoped for Larry, Joyce's beanpole husband, who's much easier to handle.

"Everything alright, Rachel?" Joyce speaks slowly, her voice wary.

Rachel introduces Gail, explains they have an animal emergency. "You're the only person I could think of who'd care." Gail starts to paraphrase but Joyce's chest swells, sucking it in as praise.

"Let's have a look-see," Joyce says.

Gail opens the box and gives Joyce a puppy-dog face. The bird is gray and agitated like Gail, reminding Rachel that people resemble their pets. Like she and Stella, both long-legged and sleek.

"It's a sick bird," Gail says, stating the obvious.

"How do you know it's worth saving?" Rachel asks, peering in.

"Rachel!" Gail claps a hand over her heart; her nails are bit to nubs. "It's a living thing!"

"Well, some are better than others," Rachel says.

Gail shakes her head. When Rachel, so angry, told Gail her boss' claim that she lacked people skills, Gail snorted and said, "Imagine that!"

Joyce peers at the bird. "Oh." She joins Gail in a cooing duet as they stroke the pigeon. The box is carpeted in bird shit.

"Oh," Rachel says. "That is disgusting."

"Don't mind her," Gail tells Joyce. "She hates animals."

"That's incorrect. I love Stella, my dog."

Joyce and Gail share a look. "The bird rescue is closed," Gail explains, "and Rachel said you are good with living things."

"Did she now?" Joyce looks at Rachel as if reconsidering her.

"Not exactly," Rachel says.

"If you could help," Gail tells Joyce, "I'd be so grateful. I can pick it up later today if you like."

Rachel checks her watch. "I have got to get back to work. What do you say?" she asks Joyce, who stares at the bird.

"Look, I understand if you don't want it," Rachel says. "It is disgusting." She shudders. "A flying rat."

Gail whispers, "You're not helping."

"What? You like these birds? Pigeons who make such a mess, the Canada goose that won't go home? It's payback for draft dodgers who hid in Canada during the Vietnam War." She laughs but both women stare at Rachel, mouths agape. "If you think about it they could be the answer to the hunger problem – a goose or squab in every pot."

Gail says, "You're terrible."

Joyce looks between them, nods her head, then her lips twitch and she busts up with laughter. When she recovers she says, "Oh, I think you'd better leave it with me, Gail. Who knows what Rachel will do to the poor mite?"

"You're right." Now Gail's laughing too. "She might feed it to her dog."

"Oh, you've met the wolf?"

The two fall into each other laughing and gasping for breath. They're doubled over as Rachel turns to go.

107

She hops into her car and buckles up. Such difficult people to practice patience on, but she's not one to shrink from a challenge. She's proud to think her patience work is done. She starts her engine, lays into her horn and waves at Gail to hurry.

Morgana Malone and the Miracle of St. Francis Xavier

by Matt Potter

"Save me!" I say, as I duck between their legs. Crouching behind them, I look down at my toes poking through the lavender or mauve or lilac strappy bridesmaid sandals and hold my breath as their chanting continues.

One – two – three – four –

I look up, and I see their signs for the first time: 'Hubbard's Hoes' and 'Dianetics Disaster' and 'L. Ron is a shit!'

And hear them chant, "L. Ron Hubbard is weak! Chuck him in the creek!"

And through their legs I see the opposing forces, lolling behind a wooden stand, young women with ponytails and young men with skinny arms, and books and leaflets and smiles piled high. 'FEEL HAPPIER AND MUCH MORE CONFIDENT' – their banner declares – 'the Scientology Way' – their banner whispers.

What I thought I might find when I slammed the St. Francis Xavier Cathedral door on the wedding rehearsal was the remnants of the parade, men and women from the army and the navy and the air force marching past, their faces solemn as the crowd waved and the music intoned and the sun hid behind a cloud. It is, after all, Anzac Day, the public holiday where we commemorate the Australian and New Zealand Army Corps landing at Gallipoli in 1915 and their horrific loss. And well, Anzac Day is equally famous for its rainfall.

But the marchers have disappeared and the onlookers too and so there's just the Scientologists and the anti-Scientologists and me here in the middle of Victoria Square.

Five – six – seven – eight –

In the distance I hear Grigor's steps thundering towards me and Zebadie's shrill top note – "Come back, ya cunt!" – so I drop my bottom closer to the footpath and hunker down.

When Grigor asked me into his office yesterday afternoon I had no idea he would sink to his knees, wrap his arms around my legs and say, "I'm marrying the wrong woman on Saturday. You're the woman I love."

Why is it always the ex-wife-bridesmaid who's the last to hear about it?

"Does Zebadie know?" I asked.

(But I didn't know what else to say! It was an unusually warm day yesterday and the dress I was wearing was soft and filmy and with his head pressed against my crotch, I could already feel the dampness spreading. And there was this *ache* ...)

"No," he said, looking up at me. A breeze blew through the open window but not a hair on his head moved, it was lacquered so stiff. "But I thought I'd tell her the church had changed at the last minute. You know Zebadie's haphazard skills with the GPS." And he blinked.

I shake my head at the thought.

Nine – ten – eleven – twelve –

"Where's the fucking dog?!" Zebadie screams, a little closer this time, out of breath and stiletto heels snipping on the cement.

Zebadie had wanted a dog in the wedding, a schnoodle – part schnauzer, part poodle – and I was holding its diamante lead when, wedding rehearsal half over, Grigor turned to me, eyes wet and voice throbbing, and said, "I can't do this." And then my head began to spin and I think I smelled almonds and I thought, *No, no, no, I can't do this either* and as Grigor stepped towards me with his hand stretched out, palm up, eyes deep and imploring, I dropped my test bouquet and Zebadie's test bouquet and the dog lead slipped out of my hand and I sort of fell against a pew and then I turned around and wobbled up the aisle and, door slamming behind me, ran onto Wakefield Street.

I guess this probably means I needn't turn up for my admin job at Grigor's psychiatry practice on Monday either.

"Where is she?!" I hear Grigor's voice, dark and desperate. "What does she think she's doing?!"

It's then I hear the chanting has stopped and six faces are peering down at me. I know I must look a sight, and I touch the paper doily practice bridesmaid's cap pinned to my head, hiding much of the brown and grey regrowth yawning through the dyed orange.

"I'm just having a bad day," I say. "Please carry on."

But then the legs part and I see Grigor – and Zebadie standing behind him – glaring down at me. His eyes are black and thunderous and his nose looks extra pointy and I can't help but see the hair quivering in his now cavernous nostrils.

Thirteen – fourteen – fifteen – sixteen –

"You've lost your chance at being my matron of honour now!" Zebadie spits.

And Grigor, chest heaving and dribble on his chin, has the last word: "I hope you don't regret this, Morgana."

Affair

by Gary Percesepe

Macy was standing on the street licking an ice cream cone as I drove up in my blue convertible. I had seen her sitting or standing or walking the conference grounds at Antioch College, where we were both attending an academic conference. She was tall but walked slowly in silver ballet flats with ribbons attached in bowties, as if she had nowhere to go and all the time in the world. It was a warm night. She wore a light summer sundress. Simple and inexpensive, it flattered her form. Her hair was a shade of light brown streaked with blonde, and the day before she had twisted a cut daisy into her hair. But on this night she wasn't moving. She stood still beneath the movie marquee, licking her cone and watching the traffic move up the street.

Macy (I didn't yet know this was her name) was alone. She seemed made to be seen. Savannah was at home, asleep, with our two kids.

I parked the car somewhere and walked back to her. She hadn't moved. I hadn't said a mumbling word to her at the conference, did not know what her voice sounded like. I was nervous. When I reached her I said hello, and then asked, "Where did you get your ice cream cone?" This seemed an idiotic question. It was a small town with one ice cream stand. But she pointed down the street, and her voice – I remember this so clearly – her voice was that of a child, a musical child. It was a voice from childhood that I had missed.

"I'll be right back," I said. I returned with my ice cream cone and introduced myself as a fellow writer from the conference. We exchanged pleasantries, made inquiries about what kind of writing we did, or wanted to do, and then I asked her bluntly, "Do you want to go for a ride? It's a beautiful night and I have a convertible." She shrugged her high shoulders and said sure.

It takes only a few decisions to make an affair. Someone sees, someone is seen. Call and response, deep to deep. The ancient machinery of desire is activated from well-worn cultural codes, the codes of the western world – the way hair hangs or holds the light beneath a movie marquee, say. The languid way a woman moves when she walks down the street beside you. The sight of her mouth, moving, eating an ice cream cone, that way women have of lifting their legs, the knees rising and the smooth tan legs of summer swinging into the passenger seat, swinging parallel from hips sheathed by the thin white cotton of her dress, the pair of legs together out of the night and into your car. A woman feels the intensity of a man's gaze upon her and knows that she has occasioned it and that it is all for her and knows too that if she wants to, she can keep this desire directed on her, because she knows how to do this and she has a power over him now, has reduced him to this elemental moment of wanting, waiting. You choose to look down from the road to see her move the toe of one ballet shoe to the heel of the other, watch the shoe fall to the floorboard and now her one foot is bare, and the painted toes shuck the other shoe aside and a barefoot woman is beside you in your car on a warm summer night and you are moving down the street with the top down and there are all the smells of summer rushing by and the smell of her light perfume, her hair swinging as you accelerate into a turn on a country road where someone made a cook fire, and she talks while

113

you listen in the wonder seat, wondering all about her and reading her face and her voice and her long body for clues and you are underway now, both married to different people, and you are in trouble. You know you are in trouble, and you know that if either of you had any sense you would stop, but you can't. Because you are going to have an affair and if you hadn't wanted that you would not have approached her on the street and she would not have gotten into your car, and she certainly would not have removed her silver shoes.

What will happen is what usually happens: the talk of family and children and jobs and bruised dreams and busted hopes, what he said, what she said, and soon enough a husband who doesn't get her and a wife who is restless but unable to say what is wrong, exactly, and the words of negation, couldn't shouldn't wouldn't giving way now to words of affirmation because she gets you, he doesn't talk like any man she knows, the idea that the two of you are in a car as a couple moving fast occurs to you, you are already coupled aren't you, and maybe a thought about time, how malleable it is, how moments can be borrowed from a marriage if promised to replace, and soon enough you are in a forest of desire and the way out has closed and you'll wander in this forest for three months or so unaware of where you are or who you were or that you have lost the way out so consumed are you and burning with new light and you realize that it is your responsibility to forage the forest and feed her now, she is hungry and thirsty and hasn't a place to lay her head at night because of you and this you take on willingly because you love to watch her eat and drink and sleep, and you scorch the forest with the heat of your love but soon enough a search party is formed and you are discovered by swinging lanterns lighting inquisitive faces from the village, and walked before the magistrate and there you are met by her husband, your wife, your children, your earlier, wiser self and everyone has questions that you do not know the answers to, and they go on asking but you cannot explain even to each other what has happened, and so you stand there dumbly and when asked, even by a friendly voice, why did you do it, what in the world happened, you can only manage to say, I do not know, it just happened. I was out eating an ice cream cone, I was driving my car home from the conference one night, and because you are both writers you will find a way to finish this awkward sentence yet no one will believe you.

It's late April now. The cruelest month, they say, and certainly it is for me. Today is Savannah's birthday. Though I haven't seen her in years, I never forget her birthday. I feel the phantom pain shoot through me, as in an arm or a leg long ago amputated. A birthday passes, unacknowledged, un-celebrated, and it still feels to me like a small betrayal among larger.

Of course, Macy's husband found out. It wasn't hard. Macy had left her journal open on the kitchen counter. He found my name in her book, repeatedly. There were also love poems.

He tracked me down. Apparently, I wasn't that hard to find. Or he had help. From Macy.

I was on vacation in California with Savannah and the kids when the call came. He left a message on the answering machine.

It was a gray November day when we returned to our small horse farm in Ohio. Already we missed the light of southern California. All the trees in Ohio had lost their leaves. We walked through the door of our home with our suitcases, jetlagged, sunburned, and cross. I looked through the bills and when that was done I played the answering machine.

An angry man with a Kentucky drawl. How had he learned the correct pronunciation of my surname? From Macy? What else had she told him? *"Yes, you don't know me but your husband has been having an affair with my wife. Yeah, and she's come up pregnant. I knew you would want to know. I'd sure as hell want to know if I was in your place. And I am not mad at you, you and me is innocent in this, but look, there is gonna be a baby. And yes, I'm sure it's his baby Macy is pregnant with, because she hasn't let me near her in months. So I just thought you'd want to know this, what your husband has done. He's been screwing around on you and now my wife is pregnant with his baby and maybe we should get some tests done, what do you think? Well, OK, I'm sorry to bother you, ma'am. I just thought you'd want to know. Goodbye."*

My daughter was fifteen. My son had just turned twelve. We all stared at the answering machine. We looked at it the way you'd look at a car crash with four fatalities. Savannah reached down and played the tape again. It said the same thing. The kids didn't say a bloody word. I reached for the phone.

Macy answered. When she heard my voice she hung up. I re-dialed. This time he answered. I asked to speak with Macy. He said sure, who is this? I gave him my name. He put her on the line. My kids watched all of this. Savannah stood next to me. I talked on the phone to a woman in Kentucky I'd been seeing for six months while both our families listened in. It went about as well as you'd expect it to go under those circumstances. I was out of my mind. Macy hung up on me. I called back. No one knew what was happening. It was a four-alarm emergency. I asked if there was really a baby. There was. I insisted it wasn't mine, it couldn't be. Macy hung up on me again.

I placed the phone in its cradle, hung my head, and took a breath. I opened my mouth and tried to explain. This too, was a mistake.

Samford's Under the Bed

by Nathaniel Tower

The sound of splintering wood snaps Samford right out of his deep slumber.

"What the hell was that?" he asks.

His clone-friend Sarah doesn't respond. He reaches over to wake her up only to find she isn't in bed with him. Has she escaped?

Sarah and Samford have spent the last month in hiding. Ever since his rectal exam, Samford has been convinced that the government is looking for him. He knows that doctor ratted him out after finding the serial number engraved inside his asshole.

Samford still hasn't seen it himself. He's not 100% sure that he is a clone, but he knows he's harboring one, and if he's screwing one every night, he might as well be one himself.

He hears footsteps pounding up the stairs. His ears tell him that there are at least four sets of feet. It sounds like either a parade of elephants or a group of heavily booted military men. He's heard stories about the clone police, swooping in during the middle of the night.

Samford suddenly regrets that he has taken such a liking to sleeping in the nude. It's bad enough to be apprehended by the clone police. To be taken while naked is just plain embarrassing. He imagines the pictures in the newspaper, a tiny black box covering up his penis. If he really is a clone, couldn't they have cloned him from a bigger mold?

He wants to turn on the light and look for his underwear, but turning on the light would attract more attention than necessary. The footsteps grow louder, and he knows they will be in his room quicker than he could pull on the underwear anyway. He dives off the bed and slides underneath, barely squeezing between the metal frame and the dusty carpet. Pressed face down against the shag, his crotch immediately itches and he wonders what type of crabs he may have just picked up.

Sarah is under the bed with him. He opens his mouth to whisper when the lights flash on and a pair of boots appears just inches from his face.

"Where is he?" a deep voice asks.

"Under the bed." The second voice is robotic, and Samford wonders if they have employed some type of artificial intelligence to capture the lost clones.

As a hand reaches under the bed and grabs his arm, Samford wonders why they aren't looking for Sarah. Maybe she ratted him out and not the doctor. Maybe she's a government plant who was just using him. But why? There is nothing at all significant about Samford's life.

The clone policeman pulls hard and drags Samford out from under the bed, his penis burning on the carpet while his ass scrapes against a broken spring. Still, he doesn't make a noise, mostly out of embarrassment, but partly because he is still clinging to the hope that they will somehow not notice him.

The policeman lifts him by a single arm and tosses him on the bed, face down and ass up. Within seconds, his hands are tied to the bedposts, reminding him of many nights with Sarah, only then he was ass down and face up. They spread his legs apart and shackle them to the footboard. The shackles are soft and silken, and he feels strangely aroused. He is glad he is ass up to avoid the complete embarrassment of his hardening penis.

"Turn off the lights," the robocop says.

Samford is in the dark for a moment before an eerie red light crackles on. The buzzing grows louder as the light approaches his body, and he soon smells burning ass hair.

The light is practically in his butt now. This is what a pig on a spit must feel, or at least this is half of what it feels. Two giant hands drop onto his cheeks and press down and out. A rush of air enters Samford's bottom and swirls around his insides. He farts, a loud trumpet right into the harsh light.

The clone cop slaps his ass. "Fart again and I'll stick the light all the way up to your heart."

Samford knows this makes no sense.

"What's his number?" the robocop asks.

"Um, it's a little faded, but I think it says '1164321' or something like that."

The hands release, the cheeks snap shut, and the light is switched off.

"He's the one. Let's go."

Samford is thrown up on the shoulders of the brute, his shriveled lolling penis flopping around. As they carry him out of the room like a naked sack of laundry, he peers through the dark for any sign of Sarah. There is a flicker of movement under the bed, and he thinks he sees a flash of teeth before they are out of the room. And for some reason, they close the door behind them.

Aftermath

by Kimberlee Smith

My mum sits in front of the telly all day scanning for news on the plane crash. It happened a month ago today, and there's still a lot of interest in the story because with the winds blowing ever since, the recovery crews haven't been able to access the turbine blade the remains of Junior are skewered on, because there's no way to stop the wind turbine from spinning if the winds decide to keep it up.

There are bits of shredded parachute and pieces of a sun-fried ribcage impaled on the blade. It plays over and over on the news and Mum can't stop looking at it. She knows it's not my husband Dean, she has intuition that told her it's not him, but instead his business partner and pilot, Junior Volpe.

Clutching a moneybox full of cash and strapped into a parachute, Junior cracked Dean in his face with the butt of a handgun then bailed out of the plane and let Dean ride that plane, in a free-fall, corkscrew spin for two minutes until it slammed into the ground. Those were the most terrifying moments you could ever conjure, knowing, seeing, feeling that the end is so near, and having it arrive in a completely violent and painful way. I rode in spirit with Dean until the end.

Junior's little old Cessna exploded on impact; the metal that didn't char just melted and burned beyond any recognition. There wasn't even a way to identify him.

Our sweet little bub Etheline Margaret knows her mum and dad are with her, looking down on her. We've tried to connect with my mum Maybell as well, but no success. It seems as if something is blocking our connection, but Dean and I haven't been on this side long enough to have it figured out. There's not a reason for everything, but for this, I know there is.

Etheline is doing everything babies are supposed to do and at just the right time. She cut a couple teeth and can sit up all by herself. She knows how to clap her hands and play peek-a-boo. But she still will never know what it's like for her mum to hold her. As much as I want her with me, I hope it's a very, very long time before she and I are reunited since there's only one direction to go in for that to happen.

In some ways she's different than what I've read regular babies are supposed to be like and look like. Her eyes are silvery amber; watery and slit like a serpent's. Not so much that it'd grab your attention, but it's obvious when you look close-up right at her eyes. They're the prettiest eyes I've ever seen, like molten gold. But they're so sensitive to light that Mum always puts dark glasses on her when they're out in the sun. She gets cold very easily. She sleeps well in the warm light that works like a prism through the glass block windows, coiling up as snug as can be.

The day I was bitten will forever be the anniversary of my death and my daughter's birth for my mum. Etheline had enough venom in her bloodstream that it could have killed her ten times over, but instead she thrived. The doctors couldn't figure it out, but Mum knew and kept her mouth shut.

This is not the first time in my mum's family there's serpent in a person. She seems so comfortable with it that I wonder if she expected the baby to turn out this way. She won't call her Maggie, which is what Dean calls her. She only calls her Etheline.

Mum doesn't have any friends, no relatives, and no neighbors she can count on, because we were her whole world after my father left us. She's spent her whole life dedicated to caring for us, and now all she has is herself and a snowballing burden of responsibilities.

Mum and Dean traded time on and off when they were taking care of Etheline. I see how one person can't do everything. Only time Mum sleeps is when the bub sleeps, no matter what time. Their schedule has fallen into chaos; brekkie at midnight, Mum has her first of many lemon squash and gin drinks as soon as she wakes up. Might be at 8 a.m., might be at noon. Etheline likes her mashed fruit, but Mum has to take the bub to the store with her, and on every errand, of course.

They eat the same things. Mum mashes up pasta with peas and makes a mush, like a paste, of fish that's on special at the market and Etheline eats in her highchair while Mum gums the same thing. She tries to hold the bub's hand sometimes when they're having tea, but Etheline is too curious about exploring and making a mess of her food to pay any mind to Mum. Mum fills another drink and her eyes get wet.

Same routine, every day, but time holds no schedule. Seems not to matter to Mum if they're up all night because the bub or Maybell can't sleep, or if it flips around. I recall that bubs thrive on routine and schedule. The routine part Mum's got down, but the schedule is a complete disaster. The grass is high and dying in the garden, and the mail is busting out of the post box. Mum gives the bub a warm bath and smothers her with kisses every day and night. But sometimes it goes a week until Mum baths herself. She goes to sleep in the clothes she wakes up and spends the next day in.

The snakes that Dean bought and sold as his business and left behind – also in Mum's care – have been prepared, by her, to be left untended for a long while. Mum lowered the temperature gradually in the room she relocated the serpents to and dimmed the lights so they naturally would be inclined to hibernate. Before their transition into a state of hibernation, Mum fed them plenty of the mice Dean raised as food for them and then put the rest of the mice in cardboard moving boxes and let them go in the bush. Mum seems to be in a state of hibernation as well, in some ways.

Mum powders Etheline with talcum powder and snuggles her and loves her like the angel she is. It's ironic, but if it weren't for Etheline, I'm sure Mum would have died from a broken heart by now. What I'm worried about is that she may perish from exhaustion and putting everything she has into taking care of the bub, and not giving a pinch into tending to herself.

I get the feeling she's going to get some answers as to why this chaos came upon us, but how and where she'll do it hasn't arrived yet.

U.P.D.

by Vanessa Weibler Paris

"Just take a look at it," says Dar, not looking at me. None of them will look at me; they just keep eating their lunch salads with plastic forks, lifting forkfuls of French-drenched iceberg two inches from the bowls to their mouths. "Just go to the double-ya double-ya double-ya world wide site and just see, okay? It's a dating site. The girls, well, they're supposed to be nice."

"What's it called again?" I ask, eating my own, slopped all over with full-fat dressing. Soggy, limp. I hate salad.

"UPD," offers Linda. "Don't forget the double-ya double-ya double-ya."

"Or the dot com," says Dar.

"But what does it stand for?" I ask. They still haven't said.

"Just go do it!" they insist. "But not here. After work. On your own computer at home."

"You're not ugly," my cousin Sally had told me the summer we both turned 13. "Really."

"I'm too skinny," I'd told her, picking through the grass and tossing three-leaf clover after three-leaf clover to the side.

125

"You'll fill out," she'd said. Sally herself had filled out attractively since I'd seen her last. We only had family get-togethers a few times each year, but the two of us had always been close. Hardly anyone my age was as nice to me as Sally was. Her "best cousin-friend," she always called me as she ran up for a hug.

"Do you have boyfriends?" I asked, wondering why.

"Not right now," she admitted.

"But you have?"

"A few," she said. "Well, just one, really. But he wasn't very nice. Isn't very nice."

"I'll never have a girlfriend," I said, and then again, "I'm too skinny." I sighed loudly.

"Oh, Jimmy," she said, pushing my arm playfully. Her hand was sticky, and she smelled like banana popsicles. I could feel streaks of it on my skin, sun warming the sugar into glistening grains that would brush off into the air.

"Girls only like guys who are built," I said. "Guys who play sports, and lift. And weigh more than them."

"There are lots of fish in the sea," she said, gazing over at the sand volleyball court where the older cousins were. My brother Jack had his shirt off. "You just have to be patient. When it happens, it happens. When you least expect it."

"You really think?" I asked, touching the popsicle juice on my arm. I waited until she looked at the volleyball court again, and then licked my fingers quickly. They tasted sweet, like banana flavoring, not at all like a real banana.

"Goddamn it!" My brother Jack swore loudly, and then kicked the volleyball pole hard before taking his place to serve the next point.

"Sure, of course," said Sally, still watching the game. "A girl would be lucky to have a nice boy like you."

And there in the grass was a clover with four leaves. I picked it, using just my forefinger and thumb, and held it up against the sun. Each leaf was perfectly rounded and exactly the same size as the rest. I cleared my throat.

"You know," I said, "I don't think there's anything that says cousins can't go out together. I mean, date or whatever. I don't think there's a law. Brothers and sisters can't, of course, but I think cousins are different. I'm pretty sure."

And then she was looking at me, and I could see my reflection in her glasses: deep-set eyes and long thin face and long thin nose and long thin chin, Adam's apple in my long thin throat like a snake choking on an egg and then I could feel it, hard and swollen, choking me.

"Oh," said Sally, picking up her Popsicle stick, yellow-stained and stubbled with bits of mown grass, and starting to back away. "Oh, Jimmy."

And as the egg grew larger and harder and I bent over and began vomiting onto the ground, I could swear I heard her say from far away, "It's not you, it's me."

I stare at my home computer screen. UPD. *Ugly People Dating.* Dot com. With all the double-yas up front.

No wonder they didn't want to tell me what it stood for.

Reeling in the Fish

by Joanne Jagoda

Damon Southeby paces back and forth in his luxurious apartment on Clay St., ignoring the world-class view of the Golden Gate Bridge twinkling to the North, and gulping scotch from a mug. His apartment is paid for by his overseas employers who have been pressuring him to get moving with his assignment to kidnap one of Anne Donaldson's twins. He stares down at the street, quiet and empty at this hour in this classy Pacific Heights neighborhood. Lately he suspects he is being followed by someone they've hired to watch him. He's followed enough people to know.

The plan is to hold the girl for ransom to be paid for by her grandfather George Donaldson – but it's not about money. Her grandfather's company has top-secret plans for the new rocket receptor system his company just completed. He's been tracking the Donaldson women for months, listening in to conversations, watching them with hidden cameras, and hacking their emails. He met Anne "by accident" posing as *David Lewis* at the bar in the Fairmont Hotel a couple of months ago, after she had been deliberately stood up by the online date he had fabricated.

Though he was his most handsome and charming lady-killer self and he gave her his card, she hasn't called him yet. Last week he put his "David Lewis" profile and photo on the phony website he created for her hoping that might do the trick. He can tell she's been on the website. Damon takes another swig of Scotch, plops on the leather sofa and wipes sweat from his face, willing the damn phone to ring. If he doesn't hook up with her soon, his employers will not be pleased, and he will end up as fish food in San Francisco Bay. They don't fool around.

Damon is jolted from his seat when his cellphone rings. The caller ID says *A. Donaldson*. He breathes a huge sigh of relief.

Anne sits in her kitchen at the oak table toying with her Lean Cuisine but craving a wood fired pepperoni pizza from Tommaso's in North Beach. She has her students' reports on the Gold Rush to read and her end of the month bills to pay, but she doesn't feel like doing any of that. The girls are at an information meeting for graduation. Her house feels cold and empty and she hears every creak and noise. *So this is what it's going to be like when they are away.* She tosses her dinner in the disposal and takes a quart of Dreyer's Cookies and Cream from the freezer, attacking it with a big spoon. She's annoyed with herself for not going back to the singles website the girls signed her up on a few months ago. After her first online date was "no show" at the Fairmont Hotel, she's been reluctant to get back on the horse. Two nights ago she got up her nerve to update her profile.

Anne returns the ice cream, then pauses to read the college acceptance letters hanging on the Frig for the tenth time. She's so proud of her girls. The letters from the University of California arrived two weeks ago. Cassie had four large envelopes and Robin had two. They knew from other kids that large envelopes were good news. They waited for Anne to come home from work to open them, and they all danced around the kitchen when they read the good news. Cassie got accepted to UC Davis and three other campuses, Davis was her first choice. She fell in love with the laid-back campus smelling like a country farm when they visited last spring. She is talking pre-med.

Robin was thrilled to be accepted to UC Santa Barbara so close to the beach. Their grandparents' trust funds will come in handy especially since their father died unexpectedly. George, their grandfather, is tickled that Cassie has an affinity for the sciences. He's encouraging Robin to think about law like her dad. George and Lillian got the first phone calls to hear about their acceptances. They are planning a big graduation swim party in June at their house, though Anne would rather have something small. She swipes at a tear. *Paul, you're going to miss their graduations and every milestone.*

Anne hears the girls open the front door. "Hey kids. How was the meeting? When do you order your caps and gowns?"

"It was OK. They gave us the schedule and talked about prom and grad night." Cassie answers but Robin is quiet, which is not like her at all. She is usually the one spewing information and joking about everything.

"What's up Rob?"

"Nothing Mom." She bypasses Anne without a word and heads upstairs.

Anne turns to Cassie for an explanation, raising her eyebrows.

Cassie waits until Robin has shut her door. "She wanted Brandon Miller to invite her to prom but he asked Michelle Frank. Anyway she's a *ho*."

"I can't believe you said that Cass. That isn't nice at all."

"Well she is and everyone knows. Prom isn't really that big of a deal. Whatev ... I wasn't planning on going anyway. There's a group of us who think it's a stupid waste of money. Who wants to spend gazillions on a dress and shoes and fake nails and hair extensions and a night in a hotel? We're going bowling."

130

"Cassie, that's OK if it's what you want." Anne isn't surprised that Cassie doesn't want to go. She hangs with the straight-A kids like her, and they do things as a group. Her sister has burned through four boyfriends in high school. Anne worries about Cassie being jealous over Robin having so many guys asking her out. Thankfully, even though they have their squabbles, the girls seem to work things out themselves.

"I'll speak to Robin."

"Mom, don't tell her I told you."

"OK. Good night. I'll be down here a little longer." She opens her laptop to the singles website and scans the forty five to fifty five age group looking through profiles. *How the hell do I know who could be a good man? I blew it the first time. Oh my God. It's that cute guy from the Fairmont.*

Newly arrived widower from LONDON. Show me the sights of San Francisco. Let's ride the cable cars. Anne remembers he was a widower. She dumps her purse on the counter for her wallet where she stashed his card.

Anne works through a stack of business cards, doctor appointments and finds it. Her hand is shaking.

David Lewis, CEO, Digital Maneuvers.

I can do this. I'll call him. But not tonight … soon. She covers her eyes with her hands. *Anne, get a grip! Stop being a wimp.* She grabs her cell phone charging on the counter. She punches in the number. It rings four times, and she almost disconnects. Then she hears his English accent.

"Good evening."

"Hello, is this David?"

"David Lewis speaking."

"This is Anne. I don't know if you remember me. We met at the Fairmont last month."

"Oh most definitely. You were that attractive widow drinking a Cosmo."

Anne acts casual but she is chewing her nails. "How have you been, David?"

131

"I've been swamped … terribly busy with setting up my new office."

She decides to go for it. "David, if you've got time, I'd like to show you around San Francisco." She doesn't let on she saw his profile on the website.

"That sounds lovely. Let me check my calendar. How about Sunday?"

"That works for me. Let's meet at the information booth at Pier 39 at 11AM. I'll plan a few things for us."

"It's a date Anne, but can you tell me your last name and is the number here on my phone one I can use in case of an emergency?"

She almost giggles, biting her lip. "I'm Anne Donaldson, and yes I called you on my cell. See you Sunday. Good night."

"Sleep well, Anne Donaldson."

Anne hangs up and boogies in the kitchen, making up her mind not to tell the girls anything about this date. The last time was so disappointing. She shuts off her computer and goes up to bed. She stops by the girls' room and peeks in. Cassie has fallen asleep with her math book on her chest and Robin is sitting in bed studying her history.

Anne whispers, "Hon, you want to come in my room?"

"No Mom, I'm OK. I know Cass told you about Brandon. He's taking someone else. I don't know if I want to go at all."

"Don't decide now. Let's talk about it."

Anne walks into her bedroom. *Rob you'll be fine. I'm not stressing over you for once.* She smiles, rummaging through her closet to put together an outfit for Sunday, then ruffles her hair in the mirror. *Oh my gosh, I have to get my hair cut. David, David, David …*

Authors

Rachel Ambrose is a twenty-something fiction writer from Connecticut. Her favorite season is winter, she enjoys well-made Manhattans, and she loves Southern fiction. Her work has appeared in *Crack the Spine*, *Exiles Literary Magazine*, and *The Colton Review*. Currently at work on her second novel, she blogs at http://victorywhiskeyjuliet.tumblr.com.

Lynn Beighley is a fiction writer stuck in a technical book writer's body. Her stories often involve deeply flawed characters and the unsatisfying meshing of the virtual and actual world. She has an MFA in Creative Writing and currently has 16 books published.

Margaret Bingel is just a writer, living in Manchester, New Hampshire. She spends her time working at her father's beer store, art modeling, and writing (when she can). She doesn't have a website or a blog yet, but who knows, maybe she'll have one in the future.

Guilie Castillo-Oriard is a Mexican writer currently exiled in the island of Curaçao. She misses Mexican food and Mexican *amabilidad*, but the laissez-faire attitude and the beaches of the Caribbean are fair exchange. Plus, the bounty of cultural diversity inspires great culture-clash fiction. Guilie is currently revising and editing her first novel. Her short stories have appeared in *Fiction 365*, *Lady Ink Magazine* and *Pure Slush*. She blogs at http://guilie-castillo-oriard.blogspot.com.

John Wentworth Chapin lives and writes in Baltimore, where he is too frequently starting Project B before finishing Project A. John writes non-fiction as well as fiction. Find him on the web at http://johnwentworthchapin.com.

James Claffey hails from County Westmeath, Ireland, and lives on an avocado ranch in Carpinteria, CA with his family. He is the author of a collection of short fiction, *Blood a Cold Blue*. His website can be found at http://jamesclaffey.com.

Gay Degani has published online and in print including *The Best of Every Day Fiction* editions and her own collection, *Pomegranate Stories*. She is the founder-editor emeritus of EDF's *Flash Fiction Chronicles*, a staff editor at *Smokelong Quarterly*, and blogs at *Words in Place* where a list of her work can be found. She's had two stories nominated for Pushcart consideration and won the eleventh Annual Glass Woman Prize for her flash piece, *Something about L.A.*

Michelle Elvy is an editor and writer who has meandered from the shores of the Chesapeake to New Zealand's Bay of Islands. Michelle has published poetry, short stories and non-fiction about travel, faraway places, food, motorcycling, slow travel, the kindness of strangers and raising children in unusual places, for numerous literary journals and magazines in the US, Canada, Australasia, UK and Europe. She edits at *Flash Frontier: An Adventure in Short Fiction* and *Blue Five Notebook*. She can also be found regularly at *Awkword Paper Cut*. More about manuscript assessment and Michelle's take on editing and writing at http://michelleelvy.com.

Gloria Garfunkel is the daughter of two Auschwitz survivors which deeply impacted her whole life and personality. She has a Ph.D. from Harvard University in Psychology and Social Relations, concentrating on Personality Development Studies. She was a psychotherapist for thirty years working with children, adults and families. She is currently retired, reading and writing to her heart's content. She has published many stories in journals and anthologies and hopes to eventually publish a collection of her flash fiction. You can find more of her work at her blog http://queruloussquirreldaily.blogspot.com/

Teresa Burns Gunther has had fiction and nonfiction appear in numerous literary journals and most recently in *Northwind Magazine*, *Bookslut* and *Best New Writing 2012*. Teresa is the Editor of *The Lakeside*, an online literary magazine, and she founded Lakeshore Writers Workshop in Oakland, California where she leads creative writing workshops and classes and works one-on-one with writers. Find her work at http://www.teresaburnsgunther.com/.

Gill Hoffs lives with her family and an ever-dwindling supply of Nutella in the North of England. Find Gill on facebook or as @gillhoffs on twitter, email her a dirty joke at gillhoffs@hotmail.co.uk, or leave a clean comment at http://gillhoffs.wordpress.com/. *Wild: a collection* is out now from *Pure Slush Books*. Her non-fiction book *The Sinking of RMS Tayleur: the Lost Story of the Victorian Titanic* is out now from Pen & Sword. (See her site or http://www.pen-and-sword.co.uk/ for details.) Feel free to send her chocolate.

Joanne Jagoda of Oakland, California, took an inspiring writing workshop after retiring in 2009, and launched on a long-postponed creative writing journey. Since discovering her passion for writing, she has worked non-stop on short stories, poetry and non-fiction. Her work has appeared in a number of e-zines and print anthologies, including *Pure Slush* and *Idea Gems Magazine*, and she was a poet of the month for a Jewish news weekly in Northern California. When not taking writing and poetry classes, Joanne enjoys being a writer-coach for ninth graders, Zumba, and visiting her three grandchildren in Jerusalem.

Len Kuntz is a writer from Washington State and an editor at the online literary magazine *Metazen*. His work appears widely in print and online, and you can find more of it at http://lenkuntz.blogspot.com.

Sally-Anne Macomber was born and raised in Toronto, Canada, and studied journalism at Concordia University in Montreal. Her work on high fashion and the demise of haute couture has appeared in various online and print publications in both Europe and North America. She turned to writing flash fiction in 2010, and hasn't looked back.

Jessica McHugh is an author of speculative fiction that spans the genre from horror and alternate history to epic fantasy. A member of the Horror Writers Association and a 2013 Pulp Ark nominee, she has devoted herself to novels, short stories, poetry, and playwriting. Jessica has had thirteen books published in five years, including the bestselling *Rabbits in the Garden, The Sky: The World* and the gritty coming-of-age thriller, *PINS*. More info on her speculations and publications can be found at http://www.jessicamchughbooks.com.

Gwendolyn Joyce Mintz is a fiction writer and aspiring photographer. Her work has appeared in various online and print publications. In other incarnations, Mintz is a writing instructor, a teddy bear maker and somebody's grand-mother.

Mandy Nicol grew up in Melbourne, Australia and made a tree change to country Victoria in the mid-nineties – the decade, not her age. She has various animals including a flockette of pet sheep that are thankful for her vegaquarian habits. She writes short stories and loves flash fiction. *Pure Slush* is the first venue to publish her work.

Derek Osborne lives in eastern Pennsylvania. His work has appeared in *Boston Literary Magazine*, *Bartleby Snopes*, *Literary Orphans*, *The Linnet's Wings*, *Pure Slush* and many others. To read more visit http://gertrudesflat.blogspot.com, or email him at derekosborne1@gmail.com.

Vanessa Weibler Paris lives in Erie, Pa., with a guy, a girl, a boy, a bunny rabbit and a dog. She writes things both real (for work) and pretend (for fun). Her favorite things include hot peppers, bad puns, small-world stories, and tales with a twist at the end.

Gary Percesepe is Associate Editor at *New World Writing* (formerly *Mississippi Review*) and a Contributor at *The Nervous Breakdown*. Author of four books in philosophy, Percesepe's poetry, fiction, essays, and interviews have appeared in *Story Quarterly*, *N + 1*, *Salon*, *Mississippi Review*, *The Millions*, *Brevity*, *PANK*, *Metazen*, *The Brooklyner*, and other places. His collection of short stories, *Why I Did the Grocery Girl*, is forthcoming from Aqueous Books. His poetry collection *falling* and his flash fiction collection *itch* were published by *Pure Slush Books* in late 2013. He has taught at Saint Louis University, Wittenberg University, and University of Dayton. He lives in Buffalo, New York.

Matt Potter is an Australian-born writer who keeps a part of his psyche in Berlin. Matt has been published in various places online, and he is, rather amazingly, also the founding editor of *Pure Slush*. You can find more of his work at his website: http://mattcpotter.webs.com/.

Darryl Price was born in Kentucky and educated at Thomas More College. A founding member of L. Jack Roth's Yellow Pages Poets, he has published dozens of chapbooks, and his poems have appeared in many journals. He currently edits *Olentangy Review* with his wife Melissa.

Stephen V. Ramey is an American author from New Castle, Pennsylvania. His work has appeared in many places, including *The Doctor TJ Eckleburg Review*, *The Journal of Compressed Creative Arts*, and *A Capella Zoo*. *Glass Animals*, his first collection of (very) short fiction is available from *Pure Slush Books*. Find him and more of his work at http://www.stephenvramey.com.

Shane Simmons is a self-confessed coffee shop writer who believes that regardless of quality, each paragraph penned should be rewarded with sweet treats (cake, muffins, Belgian waffles, etc). London-born, he ran away to Glasgow ten years ago, expanded his waistline and now blogs at http://scribblingsimmons.wordpress.com/.

Kimberlee Smith is a writer whose poetry, essays, fiction, and creative nonfiction have been published in numerous literary journals and anthologies. She was awarded a residency to the Jentel Arts Program in 2013. She lives with her two daughters, two dogs, three cats, two rabbits, and nine chooks on her farm in rural Connecticut. She received her MA in English from the University of Sydney, a certificate in the Creative Writing Program through UCLA, and her BA in Journalism from the University of Southern

California. She is enrolled currently in post-graduate studies at Columbia University in New York. She can do a headstand on a trampoline, kill a chook, and make hard cider from the apples in her orchard.

Andrew Stancek was born in Bratislava and saw Russian tanks occupying his homeland. His dreams of circuses and ice cream, flying and lion-taming, miracle and romance have appeared recently in print in *LA Review*, *Windsor Review* and *New Sun Rising: Stories for Japan*. Among the many online publications featuring his work are *Every Day Fiction*, *Gemini Magazine* (Flash Fiction Contest Grand Prize Winner), *fwriction*, *r.kv.r.y. quarterly literary journal*, *Tin House*, *Flash Fiction Chronicles*, *The Linnet's Wings*, *Connotation Press*, *THIS Literary Magazine*, *LA Review*, *Windsor Review*, *Thrice Fiction Magazine*, *New Sun Rising*, and *Pure Slush* online.

Susan Tepper is the author of four published books of fiction and a chapbook of poetry. Her most recent title *The Merrill Diaries* (*Pure Slush Books*, July 2013) is a Novel in Stories that follows a young woman's adventures in love and lust on two continents, spanning a decade. Tepper has received nine Pushcart nominations, and one for the Pulitzer Prize in fiction. You can visit her website here: http://www.susantepper.com.

Nathaniel Tower lives in the Twin Cities with his wife and daughter. After teaching high school English for nine years, he decided to pursue a career in writing / publishing / editing. His fiction has appeared in over two hundred online and print journals. His first collection of fiction, *Nagging Wives, Foolish Husbands*, was released in 2013 through *Martian Lit*. Nathaniel is the founding and managing editor of *Bartleby Snopes Literary Magazine and Press*. You can find out more about Nathaniel at http://nathanieltower.wordpress.com.

Townsend Walker lives in San Francisco. His stories have been published in over fifty literary journals and included in seven anthologies. One story won the SLO NightWriters story contest. Two were nominated for the PEN / O. Henry Award. Four were performed at the New Short Fiction Series in Hollywood. He is associate editor at *Grey Sparrow Journal*. During a career in finance he published three books, on foreign exchange, derivatives and portfolio management. Educated at Georgetown, NYU and Stanford, his website is at http://www.townsendwalker.com.

Michael Webb is continually surprised anyone is interested in what he has to say, and he blogs occasionally at http://innocentsaccidentshints.blogspot.com.

Other volumes in the *2014* series from Pure Slush

Visit the Pure Slush Store:
http://pureslush.webs.com/store.htm

January 2014 Vol. 1
ISBN: 978-1-925101-03-4

February 2014 Vol. 2
ISBN: 978-1-925101-14-0

March 2014 Vol. 3
ISBN: 978-1-925101-17-1

May 2014 Vol. 5
ISBN: 978-1-925101-30-0

June 2014 Vol. 6
ISBN: 978-1-925101-34-8

July 2014 Vol. 7
ISBN: 978-1-925101-37-9